SEE THEM DIE

Dr Hamlet Mottrell Series
Book One

Michael Fowler

SAPERE
BOOKS

SEE THEM DIE

Published by Sapere Books.

20 Windermere Drive, Leeds, England, LS17 7UZ,
United Kingdom

saperebooks.com

ISBN: 978-1-80055-581-5

ONE

Three years later

'In 400 yards you have reached your destination.'

DS Alix Rainbow slowed the car and checked the satnav again, her face creasing into a frown. She was a mile outside the village of Cadeby and all she could see was swathes of lush farmland either side of the road. Not a house in sight. *The location has to be wrong,* she told herself, slowing the car further as she approached a sharp left-hand bend. As she took it, she spotted a wide layby beside dense woodland on her nearside and yanking the steering and braking heavily she pulled into it and came to a halt.

She saw a narrow road branching away from the carriageway. It ran beneath an old railway tunnel, disappearing into a bend and the only thing facing her was a bank of thick mature trees that offered up very little sunlight. In front of her, the road swung right, vanishing behind high hedges, where a roadside sign told her the village of Sprotbrough lay a mile up the road. Looking at the satnav again, she arrived at the conclusion that she had either put in the wrong coordinates or been given the wrong postcode.

'Are you sure this is right?' asked DI Lauren Simmerson, looking around from the passenger seat.

Alix met her boss's gaze. 'This is the postcode I scribbled down when he phoned me.' Alix took another look around. For the first time she noticed that the layby they had pulled into was the beginning of a track that led into woodland, where a five-bar wooden gate barred the way. Upon it was a large weathered sign and, straining her eyes, she could just make out the words, 'Trespassers will be shot'. The word 'prosecuted' had been crossed out. Had the setting not been so eerie the sign would have amused her.

'I'll give him a ring,' she said, pulling aside her seat belt and reaching behind for her bag on the back seat. Opening it, she fished out her mobile and activated it, letting out a heavy sigh as she viewed the screen. 'Oh, that's just great. We're in the middle of nowhere and there's no flaming signal.'

'I'll try mine,' said Lauren, reaching into the footwell where her own bag lay.

The sudden bang on the roof startled them both and they whipped sideways to see a dishevelled-looking man, face pressed against the passenger window, staring in at them.

Alix's heart jumped a beat. The man had appeared from nowhere.

'Detective Sergeant Rainbow?' the man shouted through the closed window, fixing them with sapphire-blue eyes and indicating for the window to be wound down.

Alix viewed their visitor, quickly recognising him, though he no longer looked like the man she had seen three years ago. The eyes still had that warmth about them, despite the penetrating glare he was currently giving, but his hair had grown somewhat since they had last spoken, now tumbling over his collar with uncombed straggly ends. He also had several day's beard growth on his face that she couldn't help but think made him look a lot older than his thirty-five years. She powered down the window. 'Dr Mottrell.'

'You found me then?'

She nodded. 'I was just thinking I'd got the wrong location.' She glanced swiftly around her, returning her gaze to lock eyes with the former forensic psychologist. 'You live here?' she asked.

He nodded, dropping the forceful look and replacing it with a smile. 'Yes, my place is a couple of hundred yards up there.' He dipped his head back to the gate. 'To be honest, I wasn't sure whether you would come or not.'

'You said you needed to talk to us about an unsolved murder in Derbyshire?'

Hamlet Mottrell had rung Alix late the previous day. Initially she had hesitated in speaking with him as he was officially still a suspect in an unsolved murder, but then he had blurted out, 'I think someone's been murdered and I think it could be linked to my case'. He had insisted on speaking with her urgently, giving her his location before hanging up.

Her curiosity aroused she went to her computer and immediately checked out current murder investigations in Derbyshire and found three. One was a stabbing outside a bar following a drunken fight between a group of men. The second was domestic related, where the husband had beaten the living daylights out of his wife before strangling her, and the third one had been launched following the discovery of human bones on Eyam Moor a week ago.

She had scrolled down that last incident and the update was showing that the bones were now believed to have lain there for well over a hundred years and were awaiting examination by a forensic anthropologist. Unsure how any of them could be related to Hamlet's case she had run the conversation past Lauren, and after talking it through, her boss had decided there would be nothing to lose by talking with him, telling her she would tag along to witness what he had to say.

Alix said now, 'I wasn't sure whether to come or not, either. My boss has made that decision. I hope for your sake you've not led us here on a wild-goose chase, otherwise I'll have your guts for garters.'

Hamlet studied Alix's face for a moment and then said, 'I wouldn't dream of it, Detective. What I have to tell you might help you with your investigation into the murder of my family.' He paused for a moment as if unsure what to say next. Following several seconds of silence, he said calmly, 'I'm not wasting your time, I assure you.'

She switched her gaze to her DI.

Lauren shrugged her shoulders, offering up a 'what have we got to lose' look.

Alix returned her gaze, eyeing Hamlet with scepticism. His wife Helen, and unborn daughter, together with those of his adopted parents, Robert and Mary, were names presently added to those on the nations unsolved murder list, and although the case was currently closed, Hamlet was still their major suspect, despite the Crown Prosecution Service determining that there wasn't enough evidence to take him to court.

Throughout the numerous interviews she'd had with him, he had never given satisfactory answers to any of the questions relating to the killings of his wife and unborn child, continually alleging that someone had attacked him and knocked him out and that he couldn't remember anything. And, while he had no alibi for the time of the killings, because he had been at home with them, he did have an alibi for the time his parents were killed. A rock-solid one. Both his next-door neighbours had told her they had been chatting with him whilst he had been gardening.

Their enquiry had looked at the possibility of Hamlet having an accomplice but after six months of searching and not finding one the CPS had reluctantly erred on the side of caution and ordered Alix to release him from custody until such time as there was sufficient evidence to charge. That decision had felt like a slap in the face after all the effort Alix had put into the investigation and she had been determined to bring the case against Hamlet to a solid conclusion. She had spent several months working back through the evidence hoping for a breakthrough, but, despite her best efforts, that hadn't come.

Now, three years later, it was Alix's suspicion that Hamlet's phone call was a ruse to probe into what was happening with the investigation, and she had run that notion past her DCI after receiving his call, expressing her concerns about visiting him. Karl Henry Jackson had thought about it and told her to follow up with Hamlet, telling her, 'There's no harm in hearing what he has to say,' and adding with a smirk, 'and see if you can beat a confession out of him while you're at it.'

'Come on, I won't bite,' Hamlet said now, turning his back on them and setting off up the track toward the gate.

Hamlet opened the gate for them to drive through, and as they passed, he called for them to wait while he closed it, securing it with a chain.

As Alix stopped beneath the canopy of trees that offered very little in the way of light she suddenly felt uncomfortable. *He's locking our escape route!* Even though she had Lauren as back-up, and the office knew where they were going and with whom they were meeting, the bottom line was that they would be no match for someone who she believed had murdered at least two people, maybe four, and they were in a place that would take an eternity to find should they put out a distress call.

Hamlet jumped into the back seat, rocking the car.

Alix looked over her shoulder. The man smelled of damp and the long coat he had on looked like it had been slept in. Studying his weather-beaten face, she couldn't help but think that anyone meeting Hamlet for the first time would assume he was a tramp rather than a highly educated man with a doctoral degree in psychology.

'We go up this track for about quarter of a mile. You'll come to a clearing on your right,' he said, pointing up ahead.

The track was narrow and full of ruts that severely tested the car's suspension.

Thirty seconds later, Hamlet called out, 'We're here.'

The trees had opened up and it was no longer gloomy. Bright daylight poured down from above, and Alix pulled on the steering wheel, turning into a clearing the size of half a football pitch. She got her first sight of Hamlet Mottrell's residence. It was a single-storey log cabin with pitched roof and a stone chimney poking through the centre. The roof extended over the front, supported by two stone pillars — one either end — and beneath it there was a veranda with wrap-around railings. At one time the cabin had been painted green, but that was now weathered and blistered and Alix couldn't help but think that given a fresh coat of paint this place would look breath-taking. The rural setting was certainly idyllic.

As if echoing Alix's thoughts, Lauren Simmerson exclaimed, 'Wow, this is stunning.'

'Not bad is it,' Hamlet responded, opening the back door and swinging out his legs, 'especially if you have to live the forced life of a recluse.'

While she didn't want to get too friendly with him, keeping matters on a professional footing, Alix couldn't resist asking, 'How did you come by this place?' as she turned off the engine and followed Hamlet out of the car.

He was making for the veranda. Alix noticed a small round table with two chairs set next to a pair of French doors that was the entranceway into the cabin. A mug was on the table and a bowl beneath it.

He stopped on the porch and half-turned. 'It belonged to my grandfather.' He paused. 'Well, my adopted grandfather, as I've been continually reminded since the murders, but he was the only grandfather I knew. In his spare time, he was an artist. A good one. He exhibited in London regularly. When he retired, he bought this place as somewhere he could come and paint in peace and quiet — he used to bring me here and we'd spend weekends together. I have some very happy memories here.' He paused again, his gaze going skywards.

Alix watched his face change to one which was solemn and thoughtful-looking.

'He left it to me when he died. I had some work done on it when I married Helen and we used it whenever we could.' Hamlet again went quiet. 'I deserted this place after Helen's death, but after I was told my services were no longer required at the unit, and the press continued hounding me and my neighbours no longer talked to me, well, I decided it was the best option I had of staying out of the limelight.' He gave a nervous half-laugh, turned and made for the doors. 'Come, I'll show you the place and then I'll explain why I called you.'

The instant Hamlet opened one of the French doors, the head of a small wire-haired terrier dog appeared, yapping ten-to-the-dozen, and before he could put a foot in the gap it had squirmed through, its tail windmilling. Hamlet grabbed its collar, scooping it up before it could reach the two detectives who had stopped in their tracks. 'Hello boy,' he said, letting the dog excitedly lick his rough-haired chin. Pulling him away from his face, pointing him toward Alix and Lauren, he added, 'Meet my best friend, Lucky. I found him eight months ago during one of my walks along the canal. He was tied up in a sack but thankfully it hadn't sunk. Someone had tried to drown him. Hence his name.' He set the dog down and tapped its backside, 'Go on boy, inside. Chair.'

The terrier scampered back inside and Hamlet stood to one side, sweeping forward a hand to welcome the detectives into his home.

Alix stepped into the cabin, quickly taking in the surroundings. She half-expected to see animal heads hung up on the walls, but saw only varnished wood that was dulled with age. The lounge and dining room were one and the space was filled with furniture that had seen better days. There was a musty smell that she couldn't identify and guessed it came from the dog, whom she saw was now hunkered down in a sagging armchair, its large brown eyes fixed on her. She had never been fond of dogs since a neighbour's collie had got through a hole in their adjoining hedge and nipped her when she was young.

Pulling her gaze away, she cast her eyes around the room. Its focal point was an inglenook, soot-stained, stone fireplace in which was set a large iron grate with the residues of a fire. She could now detect woodsmoke among the musty smell. Threadbare rugs covered the floor. Alix guessed nothing had been added since Hamlet's grandfather had furnished the place, except for some of the pictures on the walls. Among several old-looking landscape paintings, she recognised family photographs from Hamlet's home in Arbourthorne at the time of the murders, most of them of him and his wife, Helen.

'Can I get you both a drink?'

Hamlet's voice brought back Alix's gaze. She looked to her DI.

'It may be a cabin in the woods, but I do have running water and electricity,' he said with a smile, showing off surprisingly white teeth.

At least he was cleaning those regularly, Alix thought. She wasn't keen on hanging around too long and, declining the offer as politely as she could, said, 'You wanted to tell us about a murder in Derbyshire?'

Lauren, however, took up the offer of coffee and Hamlet disappeared into the kitchen, returning five minutes later with two coffees that he set down on the dining table. Pushing some clutter to one side, he slipped out a rolled-up sheet of paper from under his arm and joined the two seated detectives.

TWO

As Hamlet lingered over Alix's face, studying her features, he could see she hadn't changed much in the three years since he'd last faced her across the interview table at the police station. Then, he recalled, her dark brown hair had been fashioned into a tight bob, the ends tucked into her neck, with a fringe that she kept sweeping away from her right eye, so she could continue fixing him with those probing brown eyes, checking for his reaction when she'd asked him for the umpteenth time, 'Did you kill your wife and unborn child? Did you kill your adopted parents? Just get it off your chest, you'll feel better.' Now he saw that it was slightly longer, resting on her shoulders, and the annoying fringe had grown out, forming part of its flowing style. It looked better, he thought. Softened her face, despite the look she was currently giving him. *That stone-faced stare hasn't changed at all.* Seeing that look triggered memories. Bad ones. *My life has changed so much since I last saw you.* His heart skipped a beat and he could feel a band of panic tightening around his chest. He took a deep breath.

'Well, it's been a while since I last saw you,' Alix said.

Hamlet noted that she didn't blink when she said that. *Was that greeting a taunt?* The clamp around his chest suddenly got tighter.

She followed it up with, 'How've you been coping?'

Hamlet took another sharp breath and held it. These were techniques he had used in the past to settle his patients and help them relax, so they could feel comfortable before they off-loaded their troubles. *Or confessed.* He slowly released the breath. 'It's not easy having to cope with still being labelled a killer.'

'No, I guess not.'

She still hadn't blinked, though he now sensed some kind of unease in her. In that moment he wondered if she too was revisiting the many hours of grilling she had given him. The interrogation was as fresh in his head as if it had just finished.

'Now what about this murder in Derbyshire?'

Lauren's interjection diverted his thoughts and Hamlet switched his focus upon her. He could see that she'd also not changed much. Her hair was still the same; long, streaked blonde, with a straight fringe that teased the top of her neatly plucked eyebrows. Those grey-blue eyes still glistened, giving away the softness within her despite the nondescript stare she was currently giving him. She reminded him a little of Helen. A lump formed in his throat and he swallowed hard. 'Not a confession I'm afraid. You can't pin this one on me.' He saw their faces harden and quickly released a half-laugh in an attempt to break the tension. He needed them onside. He wanted them to trust and believe him. Taking another deep breath, he continued, 'This may come as a surprise but I think the killer of my family has murdered again.' Pausing and holding their looks, he added, 'In fact, I'm sure he has.'

Lauren shifted forward, leaning her elbows on the table. 'Dr Mottrell, we cannot discuss the murders of your family now. I hope that's not the reason why you've brought us here?'

There was a harshness in her reply and Hamlet eased himself back to create some space between them. He replied, 'No, I haven't brought you here for that. I know it's something you can't discuss with me. I called you because I want to help you find who killed Helen and my parents, and I have something here which might help you.' He unfurled the rolled-up piece of paper he'd brought to the table and pushed it across for them to see.

Lauren took it from him, holding down the curled edges so that Alix could also get a glimpse.

Hamlet watched them read. He didn't need to see it. He knew its content word perfect; he had read it so many times since he'd found and printed out the newspaper article two days earlier, mulling over whether he should call Detective Sergeant Rainbow.

The detectives both lifted their eyes from the print-out at the same time and Hamlet ping-ponged his gaze, engaging their looks, trying to work out what they were thinking. Their faces both bore puzzled looks.

'This article is about a suicide, not a murder,' said Lauren.

'That's exactly why I called you. That article is wrong. The woman that's mentioned did not take her own life. It's my belief she was murdered.'

'Hamlet, you can see from this report that Derbyshire police are not treating the death as suspicious,' Lauren said, stabbing a finger at the last sentence of the article he'd copied from the online version of the *Derbyshire Times*.

Hamlet sensed exasperation in her voice. 'I know what it says, Inspector, but I'm telling you she was murdered. It's a murder made to look like suicide. It's exactly the same as what happened to me, and now I believe that this person also murdered my colleague, Dr Whitton…'

The DI stopped him with a raised hand. 'Dr Whitton took his own life. He left a note.'

'On his computer,' Hamlet answered back sharply.

'Yes. On his computer.'

She enunciated each word slowly and Hamlet could feel his blood pressure rising. *She's talking to me like a child.* He took a steadying breath. 'Can't you see a picture emerging here that shows the same person is responsible? I've told you so many times what happened that day Helen and our baby were killed. Although I can't remember anything between walking back in the house and waking up in the hospital, I can remember what happened just before. I was in the garden tidying things up and I heard my wife call me. Her voice sounded as if it was urgent and so I left what I was doing and went to see what was up. As I stepped into the kitchen, she was sitting at the table staring straight at me and I could instantly tell by her look that something was wrong. The next second, I caught the shadow of someone out of the corner of my eye and I was whacked with something. After that I must have lost consciousness. The next thing I remember is waking up in hospital, and seeing you, Detective Rainbow, when you told me that I had slit my wrists. I know you don't believe me, but I'm innocent and I want to find out who killed Helen, and my parents...'

'Hamlet. Dr Mottrell...' Alix began.

He stopped her. 'I did not slit my wrists and I didn't leave that note on my computer. Whoever knocked me out and murdered Helen and my mum and dad, made it look as if I'd killed them and then attempted to take my own life. It's only thanks to the paramedics and the doctors that I survived to be able to tell my side of things. And now I'm convinced from this article that Dr Whitton didn't take his own life either.' Hamlet spewed everything out in one breath and had to sit back to replenish his lungs.

'Dr Mottrell, I already told you we cannot discuss your case...'

'I'm not discussing my case. I'm outlining the circumstances to prove that Dr Whitton's case and what happened to me both involve the cutting of wrists.' He knew he was raising his voice, sounding agitated, and quickly lowered it, adding, 'They were made to look like suicide. Or, in my case, attempted suicide. Can't you see that?'

'If you let me finish, Dr Mottrell, I've already told you we cannot discuss your case. And with regards what happened to Dr Whitton, his death was thoroughly investigated and the coroner ruled that he took his own life.'

Clenching his fists, Hamlet let out a hissing sound between gritted teeth. 'Ian Whitton was not just a psychiatrist but also a trained doctor and I am a forensic psychologist. If we had wanted to take our own lives, we would not slit our wrists, believe me. It is a horrible way to die. We have access to any medicines we want, and if I wanted to take my own life, I would probably take an overdose of insulin. I am pretty sure Dr Whitton would have chosen something similar.' He paused, his eyes still holding the gaze of the DI. He caught the look of frustration creeping over her face. 'Look, I can see you're getting annoyed. That you think I've brought you both out here on a wild-goose chase, as you put it, but believe me I haven't. I thought about this long and hard before I made that call because I knew you might not believe me — that I was trying to sway your thoughts about me. But I haven't brought you here for that. I've brought you here because of this article.' He slapped a hand over the print-out of the digital newspaper report. 'And I firmly believe I know who killed her!'

Lauren drew back her hand from the table and glanced at her watch. 'Dr Mottrell, I don't wish to be rude, or offend you, but Alix and I have things to do. I will give you two minutes to say whatever you have to say and then we're leaving.'

Hamlet heaved a sigh of thanks. 'That's all I need.'

'The floor is all yours, Dr Mottrell.'

He watched Lauren exchange a quick glance with Alix, who shook her head, her face and body language saying, 'why are we giving this man — this killer — our time,' and knew he had to pull something out of the bag to make them listen.

Reaching across the table, he pulled back the print-out, and taking a deep breath began, 'When I was told that Dr Whitton had died by suicide, I have to say that my initial reaction to the news was good riddance.' He saw the DI suddenly open her mouth, about to interrupt him and he quickly held up a finger to broker her silence and said, 'I know what you've just said about Dr Whitton but I need to explain things to help you understand the link I'm making. Please bear with me.'

Hamlet held her gaze and she reacted by offering out an open hand indicating that he still had the floor. Returning a meek smile, Hamlet continued, 'As you know, his death was a couple of weeks after the murders of Helen and my mum and dad. Their killings were all over the media, where the Press made great play of the fact that I had been suspended, along with Ian, following the escape of convicted killer James Harry Benson from a psychiatric unit. You recall, the NHS were conducting their own enquiry, after they discovered Benson's release papers had my signature on them.'

Hamlet watched both detectives nod his way. Continuing, he said, 'I'd told the investigating team that my signature on those release papers was false, and that I could prove it because I was off work when they were signed, and I mentioned Ian as a suspect because he was the only one who was against my decision to return Benson back to prison. I was on remand in prison when I learned that Ian had been found with his wrists slit. I initially believed he'd killed himself to avoid the embarrassment and shame of the scandal, but then I got to thinking that if I'd died from my injuries everyone would have thought I'd taken the same way out. That made me suspect that whoever was behind what happened to me and my family was also behind Ian Whitton's death.'

Hamlet saw Alix raise her eyebrows dismissively and he continued, 'Those suspicions increased when I learned that Ian had left a note on his computer, similar to the one you found on mine. It was, of course, too late for me to do anything about it, because of my time in hospital, and then being locked up in prison. His inquest had taken place and the coroner had ruled that he'd taken his own life. Besides, who would have believed me if I had said anything? As far as you were concerned, I'd murdered my family and tried to take my own life. You probably would have just said I was trying to divert attention away from myself. And I didn't have any evidence. They were just my suspicions. But because of those suspicions, for the last two and a half years I've been conducting my own enquiries. Looking to prove to you that I was telling the truth. I've spent most of my time scouring the internet for any similar cases. Until two days ago my efforts have been in vain and then I found *this* article.' He picked up the printed sheet and waved it in front of them before slamming it back down on the table, leaving his hand covering it.

Lauren locked eyes with him. 'Dr Mottrell, can I stop you just there? Do you know how many people take their life each year by cutting their wrists?'

Sensing himself becoming agitated again, Hamlet took his hand back from the printed newspaper article and inhaled deeply. Releasing it slowly, he responded, 'No. I know it's a lot because of all the articles I've read. But if you bear with me, what I'm getting around to is that it wasn't exactly this story that grabbed my attention, but the name of the victim who's mentioned. And it's the name of that victim who's made me realise that I know who killed her, and it's also raised my view that it has to be the same person involved in Dr Whitton's death, and who is also responsible for what happened to my family and me.'

Both Lauren and Alix sat up together, exchanging quick glances. Hamlet saw for the first time since the conversation began that he had captured their interest. He said, 'Now I've got your attention, I'll give you some quick background about what I know and then tell you what I believe.'

Lauren nodded his way, 'We're listening.'

With a grateful sigh, Hamlet said, 'Back in 1995, a fourteen-year-old girl called Tanya Johnson, who was in a local authority children's home at Totley Brook, made an allegation to staff that a boy in the same home had tried to rape her. The detail of that allegation was that she and the fifteen-year-old boy were listening to some music in her room and that suddenly he grabbed hold of her and tried to kiss her. She pushed him away and he then pulled a knife on her, made her perform oral sex on him and then tried to have sex with her. She screamed to alert staff and he tried to strangle her. Staff quickly detained the boy, locked him in his room and then called the police. Before they got there, the boy had set fire to some magazines and his bedding, climbed out of the window and run off.

'The boy was found hiding in nearby woods several days later by the police and arrested. In interview, he told detectives that Tanya had instigated the sex, that he couldn't get hard, and she started laughing at him, so he put his hand over her mouth, which she bit and so he punched her. He said he'd set fire to his room because no one would believe him when he told them she was making it up. The boy was charged with arson and gross indecency and was convicted at court. He was sent to a young offender institution for five years, and whilst in there he attacked and seriously injured an inmate. And I mean seriously injured. He caved his head in, almost killed him.

'He told detectives that the boy had tried to rape him in the showers and that voices in his head had told him to kill him. He was medically assessed, diagnosed as having a disturbed personality and sent to a secure unit for treatment. He engaged fully with all his treatment programmes, took his medication regularly, and was deemed as being no longer a risk and suitable for day release.

'However, before that was put in place, he attacked another inmate. Beat him over the head with a pool ball and tried to cut off his penis with a toothbrush he'd sharpened. The story he gave to the warders was that he was defending himself, after he was attacked first, but the warders believe he attacked the inmate because he was a sex offender. The police interviewed him, and he stuck to his story about defending himself.

'After no charges were pressed, he was reassessed and sent to Rampton Hospital, a high-security psychiatric hospital for further treatment. Three years ago, his risk was downgraded and he came to Moor Lodge, which is where I met him. The man I have just mentioned is James Benson.' Taking a pause, Hamlet saw the two detective's faces change, and he continued, 'Yes, the same James Benson who Dr Ian Whitton forged my name on his release papers for, and who killed his escort to escape.' Hamlet stopped for a moment, taking a deep breath. He saw from the looks Lauren and Alix displayed that he had now completely grabbed their attention and said, 'And how is what I've just told you linked to this article?' He picked up the printed sheet from the table and waved it again. 'Well, because I became James Benson's RC…'

'RC?' Lauren interrupted.

'Sorry, Responsible Clinician. It was my job to interview and assess him. And from what he disclosed to me … what I've just told you … I've been able to make the link to this newspaper story. You see the woman in this report, thirty-nine-year-old Tanya Hodkin, was previously called Johnson, until she was married fifteen years ago. And I believe this person is the same Tanya Johnson who made the allegations against Benson back in 1995. The same Tanya who was found dead in her bath a week ago with her wrists slashed, and which I believe was not suicide, but murder. Murder, which was carried out by James Benson in revenge for making the allegations of rape against him. And this is the same man who I believe killed my family, and tried to kill me. Why am I alleging this? Well, because I went against Dr Whitton's recommendations to allow him out for day release. It was I who said that I believed Benson posed a danger, shouldn't be treated any further, and should go back to prison.'

Hamlet nervously waved goodbye to the two detectives and watched them drive away, hoping that as far-fetched as it sounded, he'd managed to convince them that two murders had been staged to look like suicide, and that the same person who had done those killings had also slaughtered his family and tried to kill him. He was certain they sounded genuine when they said they would 'follow it up' as they left his cabin. He'd locked eyes with Detective Rainbow when it had been said, and it was the first time she hadn't looked back at him as if she had wanted to go toe-to-toe in a duel.

He closed the gate, reset the padlock and strolled back up the track. Leaving Lucky on the veranda lapping water from his bowl he entered his home, catching a glimpse of his reflection in the 1950's mirror that had once had pride of place above his grandparent's fireplace. What stared back stopped him in his tracks. He looked weary, his eyes dark-rimmed, their blueness still bright but no longer sparkling. His hair was a mess and he hadn't shaved for the best part of a week. The old Hamlet Mottrell wouldn't go twelve hours without shaving, even on holiday. As he turned his head this way and that he saw someone who looked like they had fallen on hard times. *I shouldn't look like this*, he chided himself. Not when he was trying to persuade two seasoned detectives to take him seriously. *Would you trust this man?* he asked himself, casting his eyes over his greasy unkempt hair and stroking the five day's growth on his face. With a sudden spring in his step, he headed for the bathroom. *Time to smarten yourself up, Hamlet Mottrell. You have a purpose now.*

THREE

What's that noise? Hamlet's eyes snapped open but he could see nothing. It was pitch black. That was the one thing he'd got used to since taking up residence in the cabin, the darkness. It wrapped itself around everything until daylight. The other thing he'd got used to was being awakened abruptly in the middle of the night by the screaming. This time it wasn't from a fox. It was coming from his own mouth. Or, at least it had been. The demons were back.

He was soaked in sweat and his heart was pounding. He raised himself up on one arm and began taking deep, steady breaths. It felt like he was having a heart attack but he knew from experience it was just a panic attack. He always felt like this when he had one of his vivid dreams. In this one Helen had been yelling for help while he was looking at his wrists, where gaping wounds pumped out gouts of blood and he could see the tendons. Like always he found himself wondering if it was a flashback or just a dream. Whatever it was, he knew he wouldn't be getting back to sleep tonight. He never could.

Swallowing hard he realised his throat was parched. *Must have been the screaming.* He needed a glass of water from the kitchen and, slinging his legs out of bed, he searched for his slippers by feeling along the floor with his toes. As he stood up, he started to shiver. His T-shirt was soaked through so he stripped it off and put on the sweat top he'd left draped over the bottom of his bed.

As he turned on the light in the kitchen he changed his mind about the water. A cup of tea was what he needed, *after all I'm not going back to sleep, that's for certain.* He filled up the kettle, switched it on and leaned back against the cupboards listening to the boiling kettle. Lucky appeared in the doorway, his tail wagging, and Hamlet smiled. He guessed the dog was thinking it was time for his walk. 'Not yet boy,' he told him.

Mashing tea in the cup, he ambled through to the lounge, leaving the kitchen light on so he could see his way to the sofa, where he sank down on the worn springs to reflect on the nightmare he'd just had. As he took a sip of his tea, he contemplated on whether this one was worse than the others. They were all bad, but what was disconcerting was that they were becoming more frequent. Particularly the instances where he saw his wrists being cut, though this time he guessed it had been triggered by the earlier visit from the two detectives.

Lifting his eyes from the cup he saw that Lucky had returned to his chair. He was curled up in a ball, already snoozing, and as Hamlet listened to his gentle snore he became envious. He so wished for that sense of peace.

From his reclining position on the sofa, Hamlet looked out through the side window and watched the sun begin its ascent amidst a clear sky. By the time he had dressed the sun was ablaze in an azure sky, its ray's filtering between the trees, and he left his cabin feeling in far better spirits than a few hours earlier. As he stepped off the veranda, Lucky slipped past him and dashed ahead, his tail wagging furiously. This was the best part of the day for both of them, rambling through the fifty acres of woodland with complete freedom. Granted, not all of it was passable, there were lots of brambles and thick scrub, but the majority of the land was accessible. He could see why his grandfather had bought this place and spent so much time here before his sudden death.

He took the path to the Roman ruins. Lucky instantly picked up the direction they were heading in, quickly deviating from his forage and trotting ahead. The ruins were once a smallholding of some type but only the foundations were left now. Hamlet and his grandfather had discovered them during one of their joint ventures here in the school summer holidays when he was thirteen, and they had spent several weeks clearing away the vegetation that had grown around it, finding bits of pottery and animal bones as they dug that they took back to the cabin to clean up. Their prize specimens had been on display on the lintel above the fireplace for a long time until Helen, shuddering at the sight of the bones, had confined them to a cupboard in the study during one of their weekend visits.

That was not the only history of this place. It had a Neolithic burial chamber, and close to that two upright-stones that were the remains of an ancient stone circle. They were up on a banking, beside the stream that wended through the wood. His grandfather had told him that back in the 1970's he'd allowed an archaeological dig here, after he had discovered the stones, and the team had found the chamber.

Whenever they had visited the chamber his grandfather had always repeated the story of how he had watched the archaeology team recover the bones of two skeletons, one male, one female, together with arrow flints and an axe head and several pots containing fish bones. The professor leading the dig had said that this area would have housed a small Iron Age settlement and the burial chamber would have been a shrine, the people buried, having some important status within the community.

As a young boy this place had constantly fuelled Hamlet's vivid imagination. He and his grandfather had frequently searched for further evidence of the settlement and that's how they had found the Roman smallholding. He had never tired of coming here and when his life had changed three years ago, he had decided it was the ideal spot to hide away.

His attention was suddenly grabbed by the sight of a rabbit bolting from beneath a bush and his gaze immediately spun away to Lucky. The little dog had spotted it, and before he could call him to 'leave,' he was off. Hamlet yelled after him in panic because he didn't want him to catch it. Several seconds later he watched the rabbit disappear into a thick blackberry bush and he heaved a sigh of relief as Lucky pulled up sharp, barking in disgust.

His heart fluttering, Hamlet was glad Lucky had not caught the rabbit. He didn't want him to be labelled a killer too. On that thought, his mind spiralled away to yesterday's conversation with Detective Alix Rainbow and her boss, Lauren Simmerson, particularly remembering what the inspector had said as they were leaving: 'We'll follow this up.' He hoped they would do, and that she wasn't just saying that to appease someone who she viewed as a deranged murder suspect.

FOUR

After returning from the meeting with Dr Hamlet Mottrell, Alix slept fitfully; she couldn't stop thinking about what had transpired. She had switched on the bedside light several times during the night to re-read the copy of the newspaper article Hamlet had given her, wondering if he really had discovered something that would completely change the course of several investigations, or if he was toying with them to change their views on him being a spree killer. After all, he was a very bright man, whose job it had been to interview killers whose second nature was to lie and manipulate. Maybe he had taken a leaf out of their book in the hope of throwing them off their tracks. But he had planted a seed of doubt in Alix's mind, and she wasn't alone in that. She had got the same impression from her DI, as they had talked things through on the drive back to the office. As they had climbed out of the car, Lauren had left her with the task of following up the circumstances of Tanya Hodkin's suicide. If she was the same Tanya Johnson that Dr Mottrell claimed her to be, and her death did look suspicious, then she'd need to have another look at Dr Ian Whitton's death as well. *Not asking for much there then*!

Shortly before 5 a.m. Alix gave up the idea of sleep, threw herself out of bed, grabbed a slice of toast and a mug of coffee and drove to work, her brain on overdrive, prioritising her workload. Not surprisingly, she entered an empty office, which pleased her, because she had so much to do before the morning briefing. Slipping off her jacket, she eyed the pile of paperwork in her tray, made her second cup of coffee, and then, before tackling her correspondence, picked up the phone to make her first call — Derbyshire Constabulary Communications — to request a copy of the Incident Log relating to Tanya's death.

While she waited for that to be authorised, she sifted through the mound of files. The casefile warranting her immediate attention was one of manslaughter; only a week ago, a group of feral teenagers, who had been plaguing a seventy-two-year-old man — a resident of their estate — for months, because he had dared to call the police for graffitiing his garage, confronted him near his home when he was returning from the pub. Initially it had been taunting, but then one of the gang had started throwing chips at him, and when he had reacted, they had surrounded him, pushing him around. That altercation had brought about a massive heart attack and he had died instantly. The eight-strong gang, which included three fifteen-year-old girls, fled but were detained the following day, and although all of the boys had made 'no comment' — schooled by their parents or acting on the advice of their solicitors — each of the girls had confessed to their part in the elderly man's death. It had resulted in them all being charged with manslaughter and bailed.

What Alix and her team were doing now, was collecting evidence from bystanders who had witnessed the appalling behaviour, to determine each of the gang's separate role in the man's untimely death. It wasn't proving easy. Some of the witnesses had been threatened by two of the boys' fathers — convicted felons themselves — adding to an already difficult job, and her priority this morning was to finalise the operational order so she could hand it over to her team for them to bust their addresses and arrest the suspects' fathers for intimidation. If truth be told, she would have liked to be in on the job herself but her recent promotion brought with it constraints. One of them being that she had to take a step back from some operational engagements, of which this was one.

By the time her team of six had arrived, her case notes were up to date and she had finished the plans for the raid, and over another hot drink, she split her team into two groups, briefed them on their roles, and then shooed them out of the office. That done, she knew she had a couple of hours to wait before her staff came back with their prisoners and so she returned to her computer and signed in to her emails. The incident log of Tanya Hodkin's suicide was among those in her list and she opened it and began reading. The report wasn't lengthy and it took her less than five minutes to read through. Although the log contained a detailed time sequence, and names of officers attending, and the circumstances of how Tanya was found, the story was very similar to the newspaper report Hamlet Mottrell had handed her. What was quite clear in this log was that there wasn't anything suspicious about Tanya's death and it had been written off accordingly. She made a note of the name of the detective who had dealt with Tanya's death and picked up the phone.

For a good thirty seconds the phone rang without being picked up and Alix was just preparing to leave a recorded message for the detective when he answered.

'DC Stones, Chesterfield CID.'

'Connor Stones?' Alix checked.

'Speaking.'

Alix introduced herself and told him of the nature of her enquiry. 'Can I run something past you? I've read through the incident, and it looks straightforward enough, but yesterday my DI and I met with someone who suggested that Tanya's death might be a murder made to look like a suicide.'

'Oh! Why would they think that?' Following a short pause, he continued, 'There was a thorough investigation done, Sarge. Not just me but CSI went over the scene and there was a post-mortem. There was nothing to suggest this was anything other than suicide. Did this person give their reasons for this?'

Alix had already guessed the detective would come back with this sort of response, and the last thing she wanted to say was that they had got this information from a suspected murderer who was possibly trying to hoodwink them, or, even worse, give him the impression they were checking to see if he may not have done his job properly, so she told a bit of a lie and responded with, 'It's come from someone who knew Tanya before she was married. They've just found out what happened to her and find it hard to believe that she would take her own life like that and so they asked if we could check out the circumstances of her death.'

'Okay, I understand that. I have to say I was surprised by her death. There seemed to be no underlying factors or clear reasons for her to feel suicidal, so it was treated as suspicious right from the outset, but there was nothing to suggest it was anything suspicious. If you've read through the incident log, you'll see she was found by her husband when he came home from work. She was in the bath with her wrists cut and had bled out. The pathologist said she'd been dead for a good twenty-four hours. She'd used a Stanley knife found on the floor beside the bath. There was no sign of any struggle and no sign of any break-in.'

'Yes, I've seen that in the log. Can I just take you back on that point about her being dead for twenty-four hours. That's a long time for her to be lying in the bath before being found by her husband. Any reason for that?'

'Yes. He was away when she did it. He's a heating engineer, and his firm had a big job at a school in Oxfordshire, replacing the boiler. It was a two-day job, so he and two others were booked into a hotel down there overnight. He didn't find her until he got home. And he was well and truly alibied. From the timing of her death we worked out he was in a pub in Oxford with his workmates. I spoke with the two workmates personally and also with the manager of the hotel they were staying at. The pathologist was able to pinpoint the time of her death within an hour.'

'Okay, that's good. Can I just check something else with you? Did she leave a note? There's no mention of that on the incident log.'

'We never found one.'

'What about phone, computer or laptop?'

'She had an iPad and we checked her mobile phone. Nothing.'

'You said no underlying factors?'

'That's right. No problems at home, as far as I can gather. The couple weren't in debt and there were no health issues. Her and hubby had a good, solid marriage. The husband was completely at odds with himself as to why she did it. He thought things were good between them, and friends and family backed that up. They had enough money to meet their bills. In fact, he earned a good wage and she worked part-time at a clothing distribution centre. She'd been there six years. On the evening that she killed herself she'd been out earlier with one of her friends from work to a couple of bars in Chesterfield. It was something they'd planned at short notice because of Tanya's husband being away.'

'Anything untoward about that night?'

'No, not really, other than it appears she took some dodgy gear which made her ill and she left early.'

'She took drugs you mean?'

'That's what I was told. The mate who was with her told me that Tanya had taken some coke in the toilets, and that it made her ill, so she left.'

'That's not in the log.'

'Because we didn't know about that before the incident log was closed. I found that out a few days later when I took a statement from the friend she'd spent the evening with prior to her death. I requested a quick toxicology screen for alcohol and cocaine, but when the tests came back, there was no trace of cocaine, just alcohol. She was roughly two times over the legal limit. If it was coke she took, it certainly wasn't enough to show up in her blood. It could have been some other substance but I didn't ask for a wider screen and as the drugs didn't play a part in her death, a follow-up request wasn't required.'

'Did this mate of hers take any of this substance?'

'No. She said she wasn't into drugs. She told us that she had seen Tanya do coke once before on a night out, but that she wasn't a regular user. I did some follow-up enquiries with hubby and a couple of her other close mates. The husband was adamant he hadn't seen her use drugs, but the friends said they had seen her doing coke on two occasions. Both times she had shared a line with a friend she was out with. No one was prepared to say who this friend was. None of them had seen Tanya buying it and I didn't push to find out where she'd got it from.'

'And you've no idea where she got this substance from the night before she died?'

'Well, I did. But I wasn't able to corroborate it. She told her friend that she'd just seen this guy drop it as he'd walked away from the bar and so she'd snaffled it.'

'That's what she said?'

'Yes, straight up. A man had dropped it, and she picked it up and kept it.'

'And you don't know who that man was?'

'To be honest, as I've said, once the toxicology report came back that there was no cocaine in her system and it didn't bear any relevance to her death, I didn't see the need to follow it up.'

'Okay. Just putting the drugs thing to one side then, did Tanya say anything to this friend of hers, or anyone else for that matter, that would indicate why she took her own life?'

'No. Everyone we talked to said she was a happy-go-lucky kind of person. Although the friend she was out with did say she wasn't quite her usual bubbly self that night. Apparently somebody had sent her a text that had scared her.'

Alix hung on to his words for a second. 'Oh, that's interesting. Was it an abusive or threatening text?'

'Neither really. When this friend told us this we went into her phone and checked her texts. We found one that we felt could be the one she referred to, but because she hadn't elaborated to her friend what this supposed text was about we weren't quite sure it was the right one, but it was the only one that we couldn't make sense of or trace it to any known number in her contacts.'

'Tell me more, Connor.'

'She'd received it three days before her death and it came from a pay-as-you-go mobile. We've not been able to trace who it belonged to.' He paused briefly and said, 'Just a minute, I've got a copy of her texts and calls here.' There was a silence before Detective Stones came back on the line. 'Sorry, the list was in my folder with the sudden death report and copy file. I have it here. As I said, it wasn't abusive. It just said, 'You can't hide.' We never traced who sent it, and we weren't able to clarify that was the one that had scared her, but it was the only one that was anonymous, and as I said, different from any others she had in her phone. We showed it to her husband, and he told us that was the first time he'd seen it, and she hadn't mentioned it to him. We asked if she'd fallen out with anyone, or if there was anything he was aware of from her past that would warrant her receiving it and he couldn't think of anything that was cause for concern.'

The hairs prickled on the back of Alix's neck. She recalled what Hamlet had told them yesterday about the incident involving James Benson in the children's home with Tanya. She responded, 'Do you know if she told anyone else about this text, beside her friend?'

'No, not as far as I know. As I say, I asked her husband and the friend if she'd mentioned it before that night and it would appear not. Why, do you think it bears some relevance?'

'Not sure.' Alix wasn't going to tell him about the conversation with Hamlet Mottrell at this time. She would do some digging of her own before that happened. She said, 'What about her family? Did you speak with any of them?'

'We did. Tracking down her immediate family was the one thing that was the hardest part of the investigation. It appears she told hubby that her dad had left her and her younger brother when they were both little, and that mum died of cancer when she was sixteen, which is not strictly true.'

Alix knew where this was going. She said, 'You mean about her time in the children's home?'

'You know about that then?'

'The person who raised the manner of her death mentioned it.'

'Yeah. It would seem she didn't tell anyone who now knows her about that. I never managed to trace her mum and dad but I did track down her younger brother, David Johnson. He's in the army on tour in Afghanistan. We contacted his commanding officer out there and spoke to him briefly, to break the news, and to ask him a few questions about his sister's background. He told us they'd not spoken to one another for over fifteen years. He did confirm what Tanya had said about their dad. He left them when they were both very young and he's no idea where he is now. He said that their mum did try to bring them up, but she had a drink problem and Social Services took the pair of them off her and they were put in a home. They stayed together for a while but he got foster parents because he was a lot younger and then he joined the army when he was sixteen and he's hardly spoken with her since. He wished her a happy twenty-first birthday, that was in 2002, and spoke with her at Christmas time that same year. They'd not spoken since. He didn't even know she was married, until I told him. She never sent him an invite to the wedding. And as for their mum and dad, he isn't in contact with either of them and it would appear the same went for Tanya. Her only family were her husband's.'

'Well that seems pretty thorough, Connor. Is there anything else you can tell me?'

'Well, there is something. I didn't think anything of it at the time, but now you've mentioned your suspicions, it might just be worth me following it up.'

'Oh, what's that then?'

'Well, it's going back to the gear she took. Remember I said that she complained of feeling unwell after taking it in the toilets? There could be more to what happened afterwards. Especially, as you've raised these concerns from this former friend of hers.'

Alix felt a shiver run down her spine. 'Go on.'

'Well, when they came out of the toilets and returned to the bar, the friend said that Tanya started wobbling and had problems standing up, and she started slurring her words, and she just managed to get her to a table before her legs finally went. She said that Tanya went white as a sheet and told her that she didn't feel too good, so she went to the bar to get her some water, but when she came back Tanya had gone. She thought Tanya had gone outside to get some fresh air and so went out to look for her, but when she went outside Tanya was nowhere to be seen. She tried ringing her and texting her to see if she was all right but didn't get a reply. She just assumed Tanya had suddenly felt so crap that she'd decided to get a taxi home and so she texted her to say she'd ring her the next day. She got the shock of her life when Tanya's husband rang her the next day to tell her she was dead and that she'd taken her own life.'

The hair on Alix's neck started prickling. Hamlet's information was suddenly haunting her. She responded, 'Listen, Connor, would you mind if I speak with the friend Tanya went out with, and Tanya's husband again, just to check a couple of things out? If I get anything that I think may warrant further investigation I'll give you a call.'

'Sure, no problem. I'll find you their numbers. Come back to me one way or the other, will you?'

'Certainly will, Connor.' Alix picked up her pen and wrote down the telephone numbers he gave her.

FIVE

Alix quickly checked her team's status and, learning that neither group would be back anytime soon, rang the mobile number Connor had given her for Tanya's husband.

Jamie Hodkin answered almost straight away and Alix fed him the same story she had given DC Connor Stones, playing down any undue concern she had about the investigation into Tanya's death. Initially, he had sounded uneasy, asking whom it was from his wife's past that had raised the issue. Alix could understand his response, especially given the mysterious text sent to his wife, but she played the question down by telling him it was an old friend of Tanya's and she was following up things as a matter of routine, to tie up any loose ends.

She thought from the change in his tone that she had managed to pull it off. He certainly sounded less worried. Alix had a clear focus on what she wanted to home in on with him and that wasn't Tanya's past. She wanted to get a feel about what mood Tanya had been in around the time of her death — and so asked him if he had spoken with Tanya that evening. He told her he hadn't, but that he had texted her around 5.30 p.m., whilst on the way to the budget hotel in Oxford booked by his firm. She had texted him back to inform him that she had 'just got in' and was going out for the night with her friend Sally but that it wouldn't be a late one. There had been a little bit of banter about getting drunk and that they were missing one another, which had amounted to half a dozen texts, ending once he reached the hotel. His last text said that he would text her later.

Jamie had texted Tanya again at 9.10 p.m. when he was in the pub with his work colleagues, telling her 'he was missing her' and asking Tanya 'if she was having a good time.' She had responded with a short answer saying that 'she was missing him,' that 'town was dead' and that she was sober and probably heading back home 'after the next drink' He had tried ringing her at 11.20 p.m. to check if she was home, but she hadn't responded, and he assumed she had got home early as promised and had gone to bed.

On this note, Alix detected Jamie's voice breaking and, not wishing to heap any more traumatic weight on his already overburdened shoulders, thanked him and terminated the call.

After making some quick notes and grabbing another cup of coffee, she put in a call to the friend Tanya had been out with that night. Sally Bennett was the supervisor on the clothing section of the distribution centre where Tanya worked. After introducing herself, Alix opened up the conversation by asking about the relationship between the two women. Sally told her that she had got to know Tanya within the first few weeks of her starting work, when the section team had gone out on a night-out. Sally said they had instantly clicked, and thereafter the pair of them went out regularly, either in a group from work or just the pair of them. Sally added that she had also been to Tanya's house on several occasions and shared a bottle of wine when Jamie had been working away.

Alix found Sally free and easy with her response, elaborating on the antics they had got up to and expanding on how easy-going and bubbly Tanya was. Alix let things flow until Sally had finished before asking the next question: 'What about Tanya's drug-taking?'

For the best part of ten seconds there was silence and then Sally answered, 'That was nothing to do with me. I didn't take anything.'

Alix smiled to herself. 'I'm not accusing you of anything, Sally, I'm asking about Tanya. Was she a regular drug user?'

After another pause, this time shorter, Sally answered, 'Definitely not. I told the detective that I'd seen her only use coke twice before and that was on a night out. She never did drugs at home, because Jamie would have a fit if he knew she did coke. And I never got the impression she was under the influence at work. As far as I can say it's just those two occasions.'

'Okay, that's smashing. DC Stones, who investigated Tanya's death, told me that the cocaine she took belonged to someone else, and that she hadn't scored it herself? Am I right in saying that?'

'Yes. It came from one of our circle of friends. She shared a line with Tanya a couple of times when we were out. This friend of mine isn't a regular user. Just recreational when out for a drink. She just has the odd wrap now and again. I told the detective that I didn't want to get my friend into any trouble over this, so I'd prefer not to mention her name, if you wouldn't mind.'

'I'm not going to push you for her name. I just want to check that the night Tanya died, this friend of yours wasn't there? It was just the two of you?'

'Yes.' After a short pause Sally added, 'I hope you're not thinking it's me that gave her that dodgy gear?'

'No, I'm not suggesting that at all. You told the detective that Tanya told you some bloke walking away from the bar dropped it, and she picked it up, is that right?'

'Yes, that's what she told me. I was just coming out of the toilet when she burst in telling me what had happened and asked if I wanted a line. I told her I didn't. I don't do drugs. Never have. She did two lines on the toilet lid and then we left the toilets. When we came out I asked her which bloke it was who had dropped the coke, cos there weren't many people in the place, and that's when I noticed she was wobbling and couldn't get her words out properly. She looked awful and I just managed to get her to a seat before she collapsed. I told her I'd get her some water and that if she didn't perk up in the next five minutes, I was calling for an ambulance. I went to the bar to get some water, and when I came back, she had gone. I assumed she'd gone outside to be sick, but when I checked, she was nowhere to be seen. I went back in to the pub, checked the toilets and tried ringing her, but there was no answer and so I sent her a text to ask if she was all right. She never texted me back and so I texted her to tell her I'd ring her the next day.'

'What did you think when she didn't answer her phone?'

'That she'd got a taxi home and just crashed out.'

'Then what did you do?'

'Well, we still hadn't finished our cocktails, so I supped mine and then phoned for a cab. I was home before half ten.'

'Did you try ringing her the next day?'

'Yes, quite a few times. Text her as well. I thought she was probably still feeling rough. If I thought for one moment she had done that to herself I would have been straight round to her place. I couldn't believe it when Jamie phoned and told me.'

'Sally, I don't want to make this any more uncomfortable than it is, but can I ask you some difficult questions?' She heard Sally gulp.

'Yes, sure.'

'You've just said that if you thought she was going to do that to herself you would have been straight round. I gather by that there was nothing in her demeanour that made you suspect she was going to take her own life that night?'

'No. Definitely not. In fact, not just that night, but never. Tanya was one of the most positive people I knew.'

'Detective Stones mentioned that she might have been upset by a text she had been sent?'

'I would say she seemed more worried than upset. She told me she'd been sent a text that had scared her. She never showed me the text, she just said it had come from a number she didn't recognise. I said to ignore it and block them. That it was some crank, or probably sent to the wrong number.'

'So you didn't know its content?'

'No, she never showed it to me. I mentioned it to the detective only because I wasn't sure if it was relevant or not.'

'Just a few more questions, Sally. Did Tanya ever mention about being in a children's home to you?'

'No, never. That was a complete surprise when the detective told me that. I can't understand why she would want to keep that a secret.'

'Tanya said a bloke in the pub had dropped the wrap of coke. Did you recognise anyone when you were in there?'

'No, I can't say I did. But to be honest, I wasn't looking. Sorry.'

'No problem, Sally. One last question: what was the name of the bar?'

Alix wrote down the name Sally gave, and after thanking her, hung up.

Alix stared at the phone, her brain ready to burst. *So Tanya had kept her past a secret. Was it something she was embarrassed about*

— having no father in her life and a mother who had a drink problem — or something more than that? Telling someone that you'd spent your teenage years in a children's home is no big deal.

For a moment Alix held her thoughts there, recalling what Hamlet Mottrell had told them about James Benson telling him in a clinical interview that Tanya had falsely claimed he had tried to rape her. *Now that would be something she would want to keep a secret — a lie, which had got a young man jailed.* Her thoughts went full-throttle. *Had James Benson been innocent? Had he exacted his revenge all these years later? Was he the man in the bar who had dropped the drug — whatever it was — that had made Tanya ill? Did he hang around to watch what effect it had on her, and then, seeing her friend go to the bar to get her some water, took the opportunity to snatch her and take her home, and then run a bath whilst she was still under the influence and slash her wrists to make it look like suicide?*

The picture in her mind's eye was suddenly no fanciful notion made by a disgraced forensic psychologist. Alix could actually visualise this scenario playing out. If this was the case then it certainly placed a question mark over their conclusions about Hamlet being involved in his family's murders. And it warranted follow-up enquiries into the death of Dr Ian Whitton. She could now see that Benson would have a reason for killing Tanya. Revenge.

And she could also see why Hamlet Mottrell would be a target, because he had strongly objected to Benson's release.

Hamlet had repeatedly insisted in interview, after his arrest, that his signature had been forged on Benson's release papers by Dr Whitton. Hamlet was now saying that he also believed Whitton's death was murder made to look like suicide. But why would Benson kill the psychiatrist? He was the one who had aided his release, if she was to believe what Hamlet was telling them.

Everything was spinning around inside Alix's brain and becoming mush. She needed to talk with her boss as a matter of urgency.

About to make that call, her mobile rang, making Alix jump. It was her mother. She felt her chest tighten. She always felt anxious when her mum's name popped up on the screen. If she had a choice she wouldn't answer. She did so only out of duty. Taking a deep breath, she picked it up and answered.

Before Alix had time to say anything, her mother said, 'Alix, I've got some bad news.'

'Mum, what's up?'

'It's your dad. He's ill. There's no easy way to tell you this, Alix… He's got cancer.'

Alix's stomach knotted. 'What? What cancer? What have the doctors said? How serious is it?'

'He's been diagnosed with bowel cancer. And they don't know how serious it is. He's got to go in for surgery. His appointment is in a fortnight.' Her mother paused and said, 'I'm sorry to break the news like this, Alix, and I know how busy you are, but is it possible for you to get away from work and come down?'

Alix hesitated before responding. Alix and her dad had been no more than strangers since she'd fled her childhood home. She spoke with him on the phone when he rang, but that was strained, and she only did so out of courtesy rather than love for him.

Her mother said, 'We'd really appreciate it, Alix. It would be a great comfort to your dad. He's taken the news well, but it's come as quite a shock to us both.'

Swallowing the lump lodged in her throat, Alix answered, 'Mum, I'll have a word with my boss and come down this weekend.'

'Thank you, Alix, we'll look forward to that. We haven't seen you for ages. Your father told me not to bother you, but I know deep down he misses you and would love to see you again.'

'Don't worry, Mum, I'll be down this weekend.'

Alix said goodbye and ended the call, suddenly feeling sick and anxious. She had not been back to her former home for almost two years. The last time she had visited, she'd suffered a meltdown before she had even got there, pulling into a layby several miles from the vicarage to throw up. She had almost changed her mind and it had taken her the best part of an hour to summon up enough courage to continue on her journey. Once she got there, things hadn't improved; her anxiety had remained with her the entire time of her stay and sleeping had proved impossible. She had remained awake and alert in her old bedroom all that night. The least little sound — and there had been many in the old vicarage — had set her nerves back to the edge of a breakdown. Her relief had only returned when she had finally driven out through the gates, waving her goodbyes to her parents.

Suddenly the scarred lines on the inside of her thighs prickled against her trousers, and in that instance her thoughts returned to Tanya, and the secrets she had kept from her friend. It caused her to reflect on her own experience. Isn't that what she had been guilty of all these years? Keeping secrets?

SIX

Hamlet put the cold bottle of Theakston's to his lips and took a long swig of beer whilst looking out across the stream a few yards away. In the gaps between the trees on the opposite bank the sky was slowly shifting from blue and green to yellow and orange as the sun dipped beneath clouds. Day was giving way to evening.

Beside him Lucky was curled up on the bench, gently snoozing after their second walk. This was Hamlet's favourite time of the day. The calm and tranquillity of dusk. A time of peace before the phantoms visited him again in the night.

As he removed the bottle from his mouth his thoughts returned to the previous day's conversation with Alix Rainbow and her boss. He wondered if they had kept their promise and followed up on what he had told them about Tanya, or if they had just said they would to keep him happy. He'd give it a couple of days and then ring Alix and check.

He rose from the bench, watching the gentle flow of the stream trickle over the rocks, and suddenly a vision of himself and his grandfather sitting on this very bench visited him. He recalled the time he and his grandfather had built it. He had been twelve years old. They had spent most of the day working on a tree that had been blown down in a storm. He had helped drag some of the smaller limbs up to this point where the stream was at its widest, and held them secure whilst his grandfather had sawed, hammered and nailed.

When they had finished making the bench, his grandfather had wrapped his arm around him, pulling him close and saying, 'Well, young man, I think a drink's in order.' And together they had drunk from bottles; his a shandy, pretending it was a beer like his grandfather's.

The reminiscence conjured up a smile and Hamlet was about to take another drink in his grandfather's memory when his celebration was brought to a halt by the sharp movement of Lucky snapping up his head, issuing a low growl. He saw that a ridge had appeared in the fur along the little dog's back; a signal that something had unnerved him, and he followed his gaze to the trees opposite and begin searching them.

His eyes darted side to side but he couldn't see anything untoward, though that might have been because there were more shadows than light and he returned his eyes to Lucky. Lucky's stare was locked, and Hamlet tried to follow his line of sight but saw nothing but trees and bushes.

'What is it, boy?'

He was about to move towards the stream for a closer look when his phone pinged, making him jump. His phone never pinged. It never rang, for that matter. He only kept it charged and switched on for emergencies because of his remote location. He wondered if it was Detective Rainbow and pulled it from his pocket. The screen told him he had a message. He tapped it open. The text read *My, Hamlet, you have been busy. I seem to have underestimated you. I have also sent your detective friend a message. The pair of you should work together a lot more. I'll be in touch again.* Below the text were three words with a hashtag: *#YouCan'tHide* and a weblink.

Hamlet stared across the stream, gathering his thoughts. The message was seriously disturbing. The timing of it had to be something to do with Tanya Johnson. And the fact that the message told him he should work with Alix only reinforced that thought. She was the only detective he had spoken with these past three years.

Hamlet read the message again, deliberating what to do. If Alix hadn't been sent a message from the killer, she would think he was completely bonkers. After reading the message a third time and giving it some thought, he knew he didn't really have much choice. He had to tell her about this, no matter what she thought of him.

Hamlet called Alix's office and the woman who answered told him that the detective had gone off duty. He asked for her mobile number. The woman wouldn't give it to him, telling him that if it was an emergency he should ring 999.

Biting his lip, he explained it wasn't an emergency, but it was urgent that he got hold of Alix. She repeated what she'd already told him, that the detective had gone off duty, her voice condescending. Through gritted teeth he asked if he could leave a message. She put him through to the detective's voicemail and the second he finished listening to her voice, telling him to leave a message, he blurted, 'Sergeant Rainbow, its Hamlet, as soon as you get this message can you ring me…'

He was going to tell her about his weird text message but then held back because he thought it would sound crazy and so he ended the call. He stood, statue-like, gripping his mobile, staring at it, willing it to ring, until he realised how stupid he was being. *Alix is not going to pick this message up until morning.*

Putting his phone back in his pocket, Hamlet gazed back across the stream where the last bit of golden light was playing over the gentle ripples of the water. He noticed that Lucky's gaze was still fixed upon the treeline on the opposite bank but the ridge on his back had disappeared. Whatever had spooked him was no longer there. He ruffled the top of the dog's head. 'Come on boy, home.' Lucky bounded off in the direction of the cabin.

Back in the cabin, Hamlet put some food in Lucky's bowl, refreshed his water and then made himself a sandwich. In semi-darkness, Hamlet ate in silence, sitting on the sofa with his plate on his lap, occasionally glancing at his mobile beside him, hoping Alix would ring. He picked it up and looked again at the message he had been sent. What did the hashtag mean? And how does his mystery messenger know about his visit from Detective Rainbow? Was someone spying on him?

Why had Lucky acted like he had? Was someone hiding in the undergrowth? Were they watching the cabin? Watching *him*? He shook his head dismissively. This business was playing havoc with his imagination. He returned to the weblink on his mobile, hesitating as he stared at the string of words and symbols. Then, taking a deep breath, he tapped on the link.

There was a flicker as his mobile loaded up a web page. It was crude and amateurish in design, the page black with red writing and a few designer blood splashes in the background. The page title was exactly the same three words preceded by a hashtag sent to him in the message: *You Can't Hide.*

Hamlet stared at it, wondering what it could mean. In the middle of the screen he noticed an icon of a devil's face and immediately beneath it the words: 'Download the app and scan the photo', and below that 'Seek, and ye shall find.' He was intrigued and wanted to download the app, but he was also conscious that the app not coming from a reputable store could be a scam that merely corrupted his phone, and so he resisted the urge, closing down the page and returning to his message.

He'd wait until morning when Detective Rainbow contacted him.

SEVEN

Hamlet was awoken by his ringing phone and as he tried to focus his bleary eyes, he was momentarily surprised to find himself on the sofa still dressed in his clothes. The last thing he remembered was resting his head on a cushion because a headache was coming on. He had obviously fallen asleep, and for a change, he hadn't been awoken by demons.

Grabbing his phone up from the floor where it had fallen he saw it was a private number and hoped it was Detective Rainbow returning his call. He answered, 'Dr Hamlet Mottrell.' It was a long time since he'd announced himself like that. His throat was dry.

'You left me a message last night. It sounded urgent.'

He breathed a sigh of relief. It was Alix. He responded, 'It is, Detective. I received a mysterious message last night from an unknown number that I need to show you.' Hamlet paused for a moment. 'It's telling me to meet with you regarding something you've been sent, and it's come with a link to a weird website.'

'What?'

He read out the message.

'Are you sure it's not from some crank?'

'First of all, I can't remember the last time anyone contacted me. There are only a few people with my phone number, and that includes yourself. And secondly, the timing of it is questionable, don't you think? We met two days ago and then I get sent this.' He paused and then added, 'The message says you've been sent a message. Have you received anything?'

'A message to my phone, you mean? No, there's nothing. I'll just check the office mail. Give me a few secs.'

Hamlet heard the sound of paper being shuffled down the line. After a few seconds Alix was back on the line.

'I have something, Hamlet. A large brown envelope with my name on it.'

He heard the sound of paper being torn.

Alix said, 'It's a print-out of a skull, and there's a handwritten message on the top telling me to "scan the picture with the app from the link I've sent to your friend Hamlet." And written on the bottom are the words, "Seek, and ye shall find".'

'That's how my message ended.'

'Okay, Hamlet, I think we need to meet. Shall we say ten a.m.? I've got a few things to sort out.'

She gave him the address for her office, telling him to ask for her at reception and then hung up.

As he ended the call a shiver ran the length of his body. This could be his opportunity to prove what he had been saying about the suicides and maybe even prove that he didn't kill his family. Another thought jumped into his head. A name. The person he believed was behind all this. *James Benson.*

He launched himself up from the sofa and strolled around the cabin aimlessly, thinking about his forthcoming meeting with Alix, butterflies erupting in his stomach. Catching his reflection in the mirror, he stopped, taking in the creased clothing he had slept in and the stubble on his chin. He couldn't go and meet her looking like this.

He turned and headed for the bathroom, stripping off his clothes as he went. After a longer than normal shower, he also had a wet shave and sprayed himself with deodorant and aftershave, before selecting a smart shirt that he hadn't worn in ages and a pair of trousers from one of his previous work suits.

As he slipped on his brown Oxford brogues he returned to the mirror and took another look at himself. The man staring back at him was the person he used to be before his family were brutally taken from him, and tears sprang to his eyes. Wiping them away he headed to the kitchen, made some toast, brewed himself a cuppa and made his way to the veranda to eat his breakfast. Lucky followed, trotting down the steps and began sniffing the scrub. Hamlet called after him, guiltily telling him that there was no walk today and the dog instantly stopped and turned, cocking his head, one ear lifting slightly. Hamlet guessed it was because he had picked up on the word 'walk'. 'Sorry boy. Later. We'll do a long one this afternoon.'

Hamlet found the Major Investigation complex easily and pulled into the secure car park, finding a slot directly in front of the building. It was bigger than he imagined — two floors of tinted glass and shiny steel with an impressive three-sided glass entrance. As he zeroed his gaze to the front doors the earlier buzz of excitement he'd had back at the cabin had now abandoned him, turning into a flutter of nerves. Turning off the engine, he took a deep breath and got out of the Range Rover, double-checking he had his phone in his pocket.

In reception, he told the young woman at the counter that he was here to see Detective Sergeant Rainbow. She asked him to sign in and handed him a lanyard with a visitor tag, telling him to take a seat. He had only just sat down when Alix appeared. She was dressed in navy tailored trousers and a white blouse and he noticed that she wore more make-up than when she had visited him at the cabin. He was glad now that he'd made the effort with his own appearance.

Alix greeted him with a half-smile — professional without giving anything away — and said, 'Our office is upstairs. I've invited DI Simmerson to join us, if that's okay?'

Hamlet nodded. *The more people I can get on my side the better.*

They took the lift to the first floor and Alix directed Hamlet to a locked door where a sign declared it was the MIT SUITE. Swiping her security card Alix showed him through into a long corridor. Walking side by side they passed a number of open doors to offices from where Hamlet heard lots of chatter and a brief glimpse of detectives at their desks but no one paid him any notice, and that relieved him.

At the end of the corridor was a wall of transparent green smoke-glass and Hamlet could make out shapes of furniture beyond the glass signifying it was an office. Here they drew to a halt and Alix gently rapped on the glass door, pushing it open without waiting for a response. Hamlet immediately saw it was a plush office of some considerable size.

DI Lauren Simmerson sat at a large desk, the blonde streaks in her hair highlighted by the sunlight pouring through the huge plate glass window behind her. She rose, pointing out a small conference table set with four chairs around it, and said, 'Shall we sit here, Hamlet? Alix has told me about the message you received, and I'm intrigued.'

As she came from behind her desk she offered Hamlet a smile that was a lot more welcoming than Alix's, though he wasn't convinced it was real and as he pulled out a chair he started to feel anxious. Alix took the seat alongside him.

'Do you mind if I make some notes?' Lauren asked, flipping open the cover of her notebook.

Hamlet nodded that he had no objections.

'Okay, Hamlet, could you show us the message you've been sent?'

'Yes. Of course,' he answered, coughing, almost choking on the words. For some strange reason he found himself as nervous as when Alix had interviewed him for the murder of his wife and parents. His mouth had completely dried up. He saw Lauren write something down as he delved into his pocket to pull out his phone.

Fumbling it out he started to type in his password but hit a wrong key and it failed. His heart started picking up a gallop and he sucked in a deep breath in an attempt to calm down. He got the password right on the second try and lay the phone in the centre of the table, opening up the message. He watched the two detectives as they leaned across the table to get a closer look at his mobile.

Lauren exchanged a look with Alix and said, 'Hmmm. Strange and stranger. What were you sent, Alix?'

Alix slid across a sheet of A4, positioning it beside Hamlet's phone. Most of the page was taken up by the picture of a human skull.

Lauren switched her gaze to Hamlet. She pointed to the weblink on his phone, throwing him a questioning look.

Hamlet responded 'I tried the link last night. It's a website with just one page, with an app to download. I'll show you.' He tapped the link and loaded up the page.

They all gazed at it for a few seconds after which Alix asked, 'Have you downloaded the app?'

'I was afraid of putting a virus into my phone,' Hamlet replied.

'It shouldn't affect your phone. They are generally protected. It's downloading it to a computer you have to be wary of.'

Hamlet said, 'Do you recognise the hashtag?' Lauren displayed a mystified look but Alix's mouth suddenly dropped open and she exclaimed, 'Wow!'

'What is it, Alix?' Lauren asked, switching her gaze.

Alix gave Hamlet a fleeting look before settling her eyes on her boss. 'You know I followed up enquiries into Tanya Hodkin's death?'

Lauren nodded sharply.

'Well, I spoke with a friend of hers who was out with Tanya the evening before she died. She told me that Tanya wasn't her usual positive self, and when she asked her what was wrong, Tanya told her that she had been sent a text from an unknown number that had scared her. She never showed the friend the text and it was only the briefest of conversations between them. In fact, her friend dismissed it as coming from some weirdo and that was the end of their conversation about it. When I spoke to the detective who'd dealt with her death, I asked him about that text, and he said the friend had also mentioned that to him and so he'd gone into her phone and brought up all the recent texts Tanya had received. He found one from an unknown number that was completely different to any of the other texts she'd been sent. He told me what that text read, and it's exactly the same three words that are on this webpage — "You can't hide". Except there was no hashtag.'

There was a silence in the room and then Lauren said, 'We need to download this app.'

They both turned to Hamlet and he said, 'You sure I'm not going to get a virus?'

'I doubt it very much, Hamlet, but if that does happen, I'm sure the Force will stand you a new phone. It looks like you could do with an upgrade anyway.' Lauren ended her reply with a chuckle.

'It may be four years old but I'll have you know it's stood me in very good stead in all that time,' Hamlet responded indignantly, tapping the link to the web. It took a few seconds to react and then the downloading started.

Three pairs of eyes were glued to his phone.

Suddenly Alix mumbled, 'Matthew, Chapter Seven.' She ping-ponged her gaze between Hamlet and her boss. 'That line — "Seek, and ye shall find" — it's from the Bible: Matthew, Chapter Seven. It's a shortened version actually. It's a common phrase we all say. The full version is "Ask, and it shall be given to you; seek, and ye shall find; knock, and it shall be opened unto you".'

Hamlet stared at her for a moment, bemused. 'My, you are a dark horse. You can quote the Bible like I can quote the Mental Health Act. I would never have thought for one minute you were the religious type.'

Alix blushed. 'I used to be. My father's a vicar.' Her expression changed. 'I'm not anymore.' She diverted her gaze back to his phone. 'It's downloaded,' she said. 'Shall we take a look at what we've got?'

Hamlet looked at his mobile. The screen background was black with a bright red play button icon in the centre and beneath that the words 'PRESS AND SCAN OBJECT' — the same simple design as the webpage.

Alix picked up the phone, giving Hamlet a quick 'do you mind?' look, and without waiting for an answer hovered it above the picture of the skull she had been sent. 'I think this is the object it's referring to.'

The instant Alix tapped the red button the phone flashed into camera mode and a series of small grey balls appeared from the edges of the screen and began bouncing around. As she steadied it over the image of the skull the balls melded into two rings, an inner and outer, which began pulsating. After a few seconds the rings disappeared and flesh-coloured putty-like pieces emerged and started whirling around, before dropping onto the skull and attaching themselves.

Hamlet was enthralled, wondering what was happening, and then it dawned on him that what he was witnessing was the skull being transformed into a face; the putty-like objects were in fact digitally animated muscle and sinew, and when the eyes emerged and dropped into their sockets that confirmed what he was seeing. Glancing up he saw that the two detectives were as spellbound by the digital animation as he was. He quickly returned his eyes to the screen just as thin skeins of blue silk-like threads floated down onto the face.

Thirty seconds on, the animation came to a halt and what Hamlet saw was the fully-formed head of a man whose face was heavily tattooed. The tattoos took the form of a sequence of spiderwebs all linking to one another, merging into a tattoo of an all-seeing eye in the centre of his forehead. The man had a Mohican hairstyle with a bushy moustache and straggly goatee beard, flecked with a few grey hairs. Hamlet couldn't take his eyes off the image, trying his best to look beyond the tattoos that obscured the features to see if he could recognise the face, but he was struggling.

'Goodness me. That is the craziest thing I have ever seen.' It was Lauren's voice who broke the silence. Looking at Hamlet, she asked, 'Recognise him?'

Hamlet shook his head.

Alix said, 'The face isn't familiar.'

'Well, he shouldn't be hard to identify with a face like that. Especially, if he's got form,' said Lauren with a short laugh.

'But what does this mean?' asked Alix.

Hamlet shot a glance at both the detectives, shrugging his shoulders.

'It's got to mean something,' Alix said. 'Someone has gone to a hell of a lot of trouble for it to not mean anything.'

No sooner had she finished her question than the screen erupted into activity again. This time letters and numbers started to drift up out from the man's webbed face. After a few seconds of floating around, the numbers and letters settled into a line, with the appearance that they were suspended above the man's face. It was the strangest digital illusion. Almost 3D.

'What does that mean?' asked Lauren, her voice up a notch.

Hamlet's eyes raced back and forth across the line of letters and numbers. On the third sweep it clicked. He responded, 'S64 9NH, 23. I think it's an address.'

Lauren was out of her chair in a flash, reaching across her desk to snatch up her mobile. Quickly activating Google, she typed in the coordinates. After a few seconds she said loudly, '23 Schofield Street, Mexborough.' She rested her gaze on Alix. 'See if we have anything on file for that address.'

EIGHT

Alix took Hamlet through to the office where she worked, pulled across a chair to her desk for him to join her, made coffee for them both and then put in several phone calls. Half-listening in on her conversations, which he quickly picked up was about the address revealed through the app, Hamlet roamed his eyes around Alix's workplace. The open-plan office was larger than he had expected, with well over a dozen desks, each with divides at shoulder height so detectives could communicate with one another. Most of the desks were spilling over with files, cardboard boxes filled with paperwork, computers and personal memorabilia. At present only four of those desks were occupied, and he kept getting the odd curious glance from the seated detectives, which unnerved him. Hamlet guessed they knew who he was and were curious to know what he was doing there.

After her fifth phone call, Alix let out a heavy sigh, gave Hamlet a quick glance and called over one of the detectives who had been giving him the eye. He was clean-shaven, fresh-faced and looked to be no older than twenty-five. Hamlet thought he recognised him from his time in custody.

'This is my colleague, DC Nate Fox,' Alix said to Hamlet before switching her gaze to the young-looking detective. 'Nate, you're coming with us to Mexborough.'

Nate returned a questioning look.

She said to him, 'Don't give me that look, Nate, I'll explain everything on the way. This is Hamlet. He's coming with us.'

Hamlet offered up a smile but the detective didn't return the gesture.

Alix snatched up a set of car keys and tossed them to Nate, saying, 'You can drive.' She closed down her computer and picked up her bag. Dragging her jacket from the back of her chair she turned to Hamlet. 'Nothing of note about 23 Schofield Street, I'm afraid. I've just spoken with a detective who works that area and he tells me it's a bit of a rough location and one of their problem areas at the moment. There's a gang from Sheffield taken up residence there, and they're causing them all kinds of issues with drugs and violence. They carried out a big raid two weeks ago. Locked half a dozen up, seized quite a large quantity of drugs and a couple of firearms, but none of the addresses raided have a connection with our address. As to who owns the property or who lives there, I've drawn a blank. I'm told most of the houses in the area are owned by private landlords and it has a very transient population. No one who's decent, or has any sense, stays there for any length of time.'

Alix led the way to the car park. The car they were taking was a silver Vauxhall Corsa. Alix told Hamlet to sit in the back and he had to move a folder containing loose paperwork that spilled out across the seat before he could fasten his seat belt. As he shuffled to adjust his position to get a decent view through the windscreen, he spotted two empty McDonald's snack boxes and drinks containers in the front passenger footwell, which surprised him, and he couldn't help but think that his car was tidier than this, even though he hadn't cleaned it for the best part of three months.

Nate Fox followed the signs for the M1 in the direction of Rotherham. Alix filled Hamlet in on what had been happening since they had last spoken two days ago. She told him that he had been correct about the dead woman being the same Tanya Johnson he had mentioned, and because of that their enquiries were re-focusing on the events and circumstances surrounding her death, together with that of Dr Ian Whitton.

They travelled along the motorway out of Sheffield, pulled off at Junction 35, skirted around the edge of Rotherham, before journeying through a couple of villages into Mexborough. Schofield Street was in the older part of the town, at the bottom end of a dilapidated-looking Main Street. The houses were back-to-back Victorian Terraces, some stone, but the majority red-brick. It appeared to be a lengthy street and number 23 was roughly 100 yards from the bottom.

They pulled up directly outside the mid-terrace house and the three of them gave it a good look over. The front was white-stucco and not in good condition — bits of the plasterwork had fallen away, revealing crumbling brickwork. The front door was weathered white PVC, as were the windows, and the curtains behind them were all closed, so they had no glimpse of the inside. A narrow passage with a gate, giving access to the rear, was to the right of the front door.

Alix turned to Hamlet. 'Right, Hamlet, this is a fishing exercise, nothing more. We have no idea what to expect, or what we are going to find, so I want you to leave this to me and Nate, okay?'

Hamlet nodded back, not saying a word. For some strange reason his heart rate had picked up a notch.

Hamlet stayed behind Alix and Nate as they approached the front door, where Alix gave it a sharp rap and waited. He felt extremely nervous and self-conscious about his presence there and started looking around. A few hundred yards up the street he saw four young men in a group, looking their way, and recollected Alix's comments about the problem of violence in this location. His stomach lurched.

Alix banged on the door again, harder this time, with the side of her fist. Hamlet was switching his gaze between the two detectives and the group of men further up the road. They were still staring, making him feel uneasy.

'No answer,' Alix exclaimed to no one in particular. 'Come on, let's try the back.'

Nate tested the gate in the passage. It wasn't locked and he strode into the alley, Alix and Hamlet following, emerging into the backyard. It was a mess. The concrete garden floor and walls were cracked and weed-ridden. At the bottom an outbuilding was in a bad state of repair with some bricks missing and most of the roof-tiles gone. Hamlet wasn't looking forward to seeing what the inside of the house was like.

'The door's open,' Nate said over his shoulder, pointing at the back door that was slightly ajar. He gave it a push with his foot.

Hamlet saw that it opened into a narrow kitchen. The wall facing was fitted with cheap wooden units. A door was hanging off one of the wall units and the work surfaces were cluttered with an array of dirty pots, utensils and empty-looking cans of foreign mixed brands, most of which once contained extra-strong lager.

Nate poked his head inside. 'Hello? Police!' he shouted and waited for a response. When none came, he stepped inside and called out again. He looked back over his shoulder at Alix. 'Doesn't look as though anyone's in.' He took another step, raised his chin, sniffed, and said, 'Can't smell anything bad.'

Hamlet took that to mean no decaying body.

'No harm checking the place out whilst we're here,' Alix responded. 'At least we'll have done our job.' She followed Nate in, saying to Hamlet over her shoulder, 'Keep close.'

Hamlet stepped over the threshold and couldn't stop himself from taking a long sniff. What Nate said about not smelling anything bad wasn't strictly true. Whilst there wasn't the smell of dead bodies, the place stank of stale food, and he could certainly detect cannabis, though it wasn't recent.

The lounge was as messy as the kitchen. More empty beer cans lined the top of a stained coffee table and items of discarded dirty clothing littered a beat-up sofa and armchair. Hamlet could feel the soles of his shoes sticking to the carpet. Although his place it didn't have the best of furnishings, at least he kept his cabin reasonably tidy and clean. This was squalor.

'Hello? Police!' This time Alix called out.

No answer.

'Let's check all the rooms and then get out of here,' she added, making for a partially open door at the other end of the room.

It took them through to a narrow steep staircase in the centre of the house. There was another door in front of them, which Hamlet guessed led into the front room and Nate pushed it open.

Nate took a step inside and stopped in his tracks. 'We got a body,' he called back.

Alix and Hamlet quickly moved in close and looked over Nate's shoulders. The room was in gloom; heavy curtains covered the windows, but enough light came from the frosted glass in the front door to enable them to make out the body of a man seated on a wooden chair in the centre.

Hamlet could see that the man's arms were resting on his thighs and the jeans he had on were heavily stained with what looked like dried blood. He also saw that a thick pool had congealed around his feet and, returning his gaze to the man's arms, he couldn't miss noticing that his wrists had been slashed. Looking up, he instantly recognised the face — the spiderweb tattoos giving him away.

'The man from your phone,' Alix said softly, as if reading Hamlet's mind. 'And look at his lap.'

Hamlet dropped his gaze upon a piece of paper laid over the groin of the dead man which bore the sentence #YouCan'tHide in black ink.

'We need to call this in,' said Alix.

NINE

Hamlet sat alone in the back of the CID car watching with fascination as the police preserved the crime scene. It was like being part of a TV drama where he'd got a walk-on role.

Following the discovery of the body, he had been quickly ushered out of the house back to the car, where he'd listened in on Alix reporting the find over the radio, requesting more resources. He had then watched her and Nate don their forensic suits and return back to the house.

Within half an hour of Alix's call, he had witnessed more than a dozen cops arrive, mostly detectives, who had been briefed by Alix, and then taken up a myriad of functions, which included knocking on neighbouring doors. One of the first things he had seen uniform officers do was cordon off the street, before taking up guard, as a whole host of residents had converged upon them, many with their mobile phones out, videoing the action, no doubt to put on social media. Among the group had been the four young men he had seen earlier, and upon seeing them he had slunk lower into the seat. The last thing he wanted was to be captured on one of their phones and have his face plastered all over the news. Again.

He had remained slunk down for the best part of an hour when Alix reappeared. She opened the back door, pulling down her facemask and peeling back her hood, shaking free her dark brown hair. He saw she was holding the note he had seen in the man's lap. It was now in a see-through plastic exhibit bag.

Before she could say anything, he asked, 'Who is he?'

'From a couple of household bills and a recent tenancy agreement we've found, we believe he's called Thomas Midgley. Does that name ring a bell?'

Hamlet ran the name around inside his brain, but nothing was registering. He shook his head.

'We've got one person with that name in our system, and from the description, we're certain it's the same man. He's thirty-nine years old, or was, with form for shoplifting and possession of Class B drugs, which we guess from the smell in there, will be cannabis.'

'How did he die?' Hamlet asked. 'Not suicide, I presume?'

'Believe it or not, I am not blinkered. Even if he'd left a note, signed in his own blood, I wouldn't believe it was suicide. Not after seeing what unfolded on your phone this morning.' Before Hamlet had time to respond, Alix added, 'That's why I've brought this out.' She shook the note in the exhibit bag, then turned it around, the writing facing him. For the first time Hamlet could see smaller handwriting beneath the hashtag heading. It was the same message sent to his mobile — 'Seek, and ye shall find.'

'I want you to scan it with your app, like you did with the skull, to see if something else comes up. It's just a hunch.'

Alix set the note down on the back seat next to Hamlet.

He rifled in his jacket pocket and pulled out his mobile, unlocking it and then activating the devil's face app. As it switched into camera mode, he hovered his phone over the exhibit bag that Alix had stretched tight so the message on the paper could be seen clearer.

On screen, the series of balls appeared, speedily merging into two rings, that pulsated for a couple of seconds over the note, and then, as before, the screen changed. Though this time, a red panel appeared, which quickly parted like a pair of curtains, and the image of the tattooed man, or Thomas Midgley as Hamlet had just been informed, appeared, seated in his chair. The picture zoomed in on his face and he was alive. Hamlet realised this was video feed of Thomas Midgley prior to his death.

Hearing Alix gasp, Hamlet watched the screen with growing horror. Thomas Midgley's head was now moving vigorously from side to side. He guessed from this movement that his wrists were tied to the sides of the chair. He was yelling angrily, 'You fucking cunt! You just wait till I'm fucking free!' He repeated those two sentences several times and then Hamlet saw his furious expression change to one of fear.

A muffled voice in the background piped up, 'I told you you wouldn't be able to hide from me, didn't I?'

Thomas Midgley's head started to shake again. This time more violently. 'No. Don't you fucking dare.' He hollered. Then he started screaming, 'For fuck's sake… No! I'm sorry!'

The picture changed in a flash. What Hamlet and Alix saw now was a wrist, and the lower part of a forearm, duct-tied to the chair. Suddenly, above the tattooed arm, a blue latex-gloved hand appeared holding a Stanley knife. Hamlet just knew what was going to happen next and screwed up his face as the point of the blade delved into the flesh, releasing deep red blood, which belched around the sides of the sharp edge.

Unable to tear his eyes away from the screen, he watched as the blade began a snail-pace journey down the arm, leaving behind ploughed flesh from which blood began to spout. As a terrifying scream erupted, the victim's eyes rolled back lifelessly in their sockets.

A few seconds later the dead Thomas Midgley disappeared and a black screen appeared with the words #YouCan'tHide, written in what looked to be blood.

'Fuck me,' Alix said.

Her swearing took Hamlet by surprise, and he lifted his eyes, giving her a look of admonishment that she reacted to by returning a nervous laugh and exclamation of, ''Scuse my French.'

He was just about to respond when Nate appeared.

'You need to come back inside,' he said to Alix. 'I think I've just found another message.'

Alix gave him a quick nod and then turned to Hamlet. 'Give me two minutes, Hamlet, then I'm going to make arrangements for you to go back to our office and pick up your car. There's nothing you can do here for now and I'm going to be tied up for the rest of the day. I'll get in touch tomorrow, if that's okay?'

Disappointed, he gave her an 'okay' shrug as she replaced her mask and disappeared back into the house.

The two minutes turned into ten. Alix returned holding another exhibit bag, which she placed beside him on the backseat, straightening the creases so he could get a look at the contents. Inside was a colour photograph of two teenagers huddled together in an embrace. A girl was sitting on a boy's lap and they were both laughing to camera. The first thing that grabbed Hamlet was that the boy had a dark brown Mohican haircut, and he realised that it was Thomas Midgley when he was younger. The girl he didn't recognise. She was slim with long dark hair. With it was a torn section of paper, with the words 'Seek, and ye shall find' scribed.

'Nate found this photo and note on top of the fireplace in the front room with the victim,' Alix said. 'My guess is that it was placed there for the same reason as the note on Thomas Midgley's lap.' She paused and added, 'Before I arrange for someone to take you back to get your car, let's scan it and see, shall we?'

Hamlet activated the app on his phone again, and after a few seconds of going through its start-up sequence he held it above the photograph. As before a screen appeared and as it parted they were presented with a close-up view of a woman's head and shoulders. She appeared to be in her late thirties and had dark hair. Her eyes were wide and staring and her face bore a terrified look. The shot then slowly panned out. The woman was lying in a bath, filled with water up to her neckline. It was a boat style bath and Hamlet could see that her wrists were heavily duct-taped to the sides, palm-side up.

'Good God,' cried Alix. 'You know who this is, don't you?'

Hamlet knew. 'Tanya Hodkin? The woman mentioned in the newspaper article?'

Alix nodded sharply, her eyes remaining glued to Hamlet's mobile. 'This photo we're scanning must be her as a teenager,' she said.

'And she obviously knew Thomas Midgley,' Hamlet returned.

She nodded again, but before she could say anything, Tanya's voice grabbed their attention.

'What do you want? Please don't hurt me,' Tanya cried out. Her eyes were now almost leaping out of their sockets. There was a lengthy silence, lasting the best part of ten seconds, then she said, panicky, 'My husband will be home any minute.'

A man's voice — raspy — low in tone — replied, 'That's a lie, Tanya. I know he's away. I heard you telling your friend in the bar that he wasn't back until tomorrow evening. You're fond of telling lies, aren't you?'

Tanya started to cry, sobs that shook from her shoulders. 'What do you want?'

'What do I want?' The man's voice let out a sharp laugh. 'It's too late for that, Tanya. I wanted you to tell the truth all those years ago. You and Midge. Remember when I told you both that you couldn't hide after you'd lied to the police?'

There followed another moments silence, and then Tanya looked petrified. She yelled, 'No! Please, no!'

The shot changed to a close-up of Tanya's taped right wrist. A blue latex-gloved hand was clasped over her forearm, pressing it down. A Stanley knife slowly came into view.

'Turn it off, Hamlet,' said Alix. 'I don't need to see any more. I know what's going to happen next.' She turned away her head.

Hamlet closed down the app.

Alix held his gaze for a few seconds before saying, 'I need to get this back to the office, pronto, Hamlet. This has opened up a whole new avenue. I need to show Lauren what we've got.'

'Does this mean you're definitely starting an investigation into Tanya's death? It certainly proves she didn't take her own life.'

'It's definitely changed my view of things.'

He let out a sharp breath. 'You don't know what that means to me, Alix. For three years I've been trying to convince you I didn't kill my family, and it's taken two more murders for you to believe that someone else is responsible.'

'Don't get ahead of yourself, Hamlet. I didn't exactly say you're off the hook.'

'I can live with that for now.' He flashed her a meek smile.

She lifted her face skywards and took on a look of concentration.

Hamlet said, 'What are you thinking?'

'I was just thinking about those two videos we've seen. We can't see who killed Tanya and Thomas, but we heard his voice. When Lauren and I came by your place, you told us of your suspicions about James Benson and you also said that you had a number of sessions with him in the secure unit. Did you recognise his voice in those videos?'

'I have to be honest and say no. But I get the sense that the killer is deliberately disguising his voice. It sort of reminded me of that voice Jack Bauer used to put on in *24*. Do you get that impression?'

'Yes. It certainly didn't sound natural. Like you say, it was on the low side and exaggerated.'

'I've also been going over those sessions with Benson in my head. If it is Benson who murdered Tanya and Thomas, we know Tanya made an allegation of attempted rape against Benson when they were in the children's home together, and that he was found guilty and sent to a young offender institution. Certainly, given the nature of the conversation in that video, her murder looks as though it could be revenge for that. But what I can't understand is how Thomas Midgley is involved in all this. I can't remember Benson mentioning his name during my interviews with him. Yet, quite clearly in those videos he talks about Tanya and Thomas as a couple. What was it he said?' Hamlet closed his eyes, rewinding the content of the videos in his head, recollecting the parts of the conversation he wanted. '"I wanted you to tell the truth all those years ago. You and Midge." If it was the rape allegation he's talking about, was Thomas Midgley involved? Was Thomas in the children's home with Tanya?'

Alix stared at him for a moment before saying, 'It's certainly something I'll need to chase up.'

He was about to respond when a man's face appeared over Alix's left shoulder. Hamlet instantly recognised him. Kieran Croft. Crime correspondent for the local paper. The man had plagued his life since the day he had been released from prison on remand two-and-a-half years ago. Numerous pieces written by the reporter had accused of him being a serial killer, and he hated the man with a vengeance.

'Is Dr Mottrell involved in this, Detective?' Kieran asked, a devilish smile playing over his lips.

Alix spun around, 'What the hell...?'

'Is Hamlet helping police with their enquiries, Detective?'

'How the hell did you get through the cordon?' Alix waved frantically to catch the attention of the nearest uniform officer who, latching on, sprinted over.

'Is it a murder you're investigating, Detective? What's Dr Mottrell's involvement?'

Alix grabbed hold of the journalist and began pushing him away. The officer who had come to her aid took over and started to pull him back.

'Get that man away from my crime scene, will you?' she shouted to the officer, who began frog-marching the journalist away.

'Would you care to give a quote, Detective?' Kieran shouted back.

Hamlet glared after him, the band of panic wrapping itself firmly around his chest, sharpening his breathing.

Leaving Nate Fox to await the arrival of the forensics team, Alix drove Hamlet back to the Major Investigation complex in silence. Pulling up beside his Range Rover she killed the engine and for a moment remained motionless, staring out through the windscreen.

Breaking the silence, she said, 'I'm really sorry about that, Hamlet.'

He met her eyes in the mirror. She was wearing a concerned look that appeared genuine. 'It wasn't your fault, Alix. Kieran Croft turned up because he probably got a tip-off from one of that lot on their phones back there, and seeing me, I bet he now thinks he's got an even bigger story.'

'You know him then — the journalist?'

Hamlet let out an exasperated laugh. 'Know him! He's the bane of my life! Ever since the day I was released from prison, he's been pursuing me for a sensational story. He'd love to see me charged with my family's murders. He's convinced I killed them. Thinks it's the biggest injustice since O.J. Simpson. Haven't you seen the headlines? He calls me Dr Death. If I didn't laugh, I'd cry.'

'Come to think of it, I did see the headlines when we first started our investigation. I didn't realise that was down to him.' Alix paused, then she said, 'I hope you don't think that him turning up was down to me, Hamlet?'

'Not for one minute, Alix. Like I said, it was probably one of those scrotes on their mobile phones, thinking they might earn a few quid.'

'I'll have a word with the boss. She can have a word with Croft's editor. Put things right.'

'It's my guess he's already phoned the story in. I bet it's already gone to print for this afternoon's edition.'

'The bastard!'

'My sentiments exactly.'

'I know you probably just want to shoot off back to your cabin, Hamlet, but before you go, can you run the app again over these exhibits, so I can record the result and show it at briefing this evening?'

'Sure.' He sprang the door, swung his legs out of the car, unlocked his mobile and activated the app.

In MIT, Alix downloaded the recordings of Tanya's and Thomas's gruesome murders to her computer with Hamlet and Lauren looking on. Throughout the process Alix led the DI through the crime scene at Schofield Street and finished by telling her about the encounter with Kieran Croft. Lauren made to console Hamlet by telling him she would contact HQ Press Office and see if they could intervene to stop the story but Hamlet quickly assured her that he was okay, even though he wasn't. Then while Alix made them all a coffee Lauren played the footage back. As it ended, she turned to Alix and said, 'I need a briefing urgently. Get the team together.'

Hamlet understood that to mean that he was no longer needed and he pushed himself up from his seat.

Alix rose with him, 'Thank you, Hamlet. I'll need to get a statement from you at some stage, but not today, okay? I'll take you down to your car.'

Down in the car park, Hamlet belted up and started the engine. He was about to set off when Alix reached in through the open window and squeezed his wrist.

'Sorry about what happened with the reporter, and sorry about everything else as well,' she uttered and offered him a sympathetic smile.

That gesture bore right into him, making his throat lurch as he stifled a sob. He wanted to say something back but was too choked, and so he quickly engaged drive, and as Alix let go of his wrist, he screeched away, a rheum of tears breaking from the corners of his eyes.

From the police complex Hamlet decided to head to the supermarket to stock up, and throughout the twenty-minute drive, his thoughts were on Alix's parting words and the look she had given him back in the car park. Even though he had witnessed two horrendous killings that morning he felt relieved. Relieved, that for first time in the past three years, there was another suspect for his family's murders.

As he turned off the engine and climbed out of the Range Rover, it felt like a huge weight had been lifted from him, and he shopped more focussed than he had in a long time, adding fresh fish and steak to his trolley; things he hadn't eaten in a long time. He even put in a couple of bottles of a decent Merlot; he very rarely drank wine these days, especially Merlot, because he associated the drink with Helen.

As he paid for his provisions, he felt distinctly calmer, so much so, that he decided to check out what the front-page story was in the local evening paper as he headed out of the supermarket. Wheeling his trolley into the newspaper aisle, it didn't take him long to find the paper Kieran Croft wrote for. When he saw the headline, he wished he hadn't made that decision. In large bold capitals he read the words 'DOCTOR DEATH IN NEW MURDER ENQUIRY.' Beneath that was the subtitle, '*Detectives take Dr Hamlet Mottrell in for questioning*'. There was even a photograph of him in the back of Alix's car being driven away from the scene of Thomas Midgley's killing.

As he finished reading, he tightened his grip around the shopping trolley handle, wishing it was Kieran Croft's neck. He could feel his face burning and glanced around quickly, suddenly imagining everyone's eyes upon him. The crime correspondent's play on his doctor title had been latched onto by all the press and media during the first six months of the police investigation into his family's killings, giving him unwanted and long-lasting infamy, and was the main reason why he had sold his beautiful Victorian home in Arbourthorne and taken up residence in his out-of-the-way cabin.

As he stared around, he saw that no one appeared to be remotely interested in him and he slowly exhaled, relaxing his grip. Then, he pushed the trolley out of the store.

TEN

'Jesus, this is horrendous!' exclaimed Lauren.

Alix had just finished running the recordings of Thomas Midgley and Tanya Hodkin's murders on Lauren's computer for the third time. Also hunkered around the terminal was DCI Karl Jackson.

'The killer's baiting us,' said Jackson.

'I agree,' replied Lauren.

'Hamlet is convinced it's James Harry Benson, even though he hasn't been able to confirm it's his voice. He thinks its revenge,' said Alix, eyes fixed on her computer, the screen frozen on the dead face of Tanya Hodkin in her bath. She hadn't been able to watch through to the end when Hamlet had first played the footage. This time, she had no option but to sit through it as she was presenting the evidence to both her senior officers.

'Whilst we can't jump to conclusions, it's definitely one motive we can't dismiss,' stated Jackson. He eased out his spine and moved around the side of the desk back to his seat. 'Especially if her allegation about Benson sexually attacking her when she was a teenager was false. Her evidence sent him to prison. You could also accept revenge as a motive behind the murder of Hamlet's wife, because Benson was about to be sent back to prison following Hamlet's assessment of him; however, tracking down and killing Hamlet's adopted parents as well seems more than a bit extreme.'

'Hamlet told us that Benson was diagnosed with a personality disorder,' interjected Alix.

'The guy has to be a full-on psycho to have done this,' mumbled Jackson, shaking his head. 'Didn't you say that Hamlet also believes that Benson murdered Dr Whitton?' Before Alix could respond, Jackson continued, 'Why would he murder Dr Whitton? He helped him to escape from Moor Lodge, if it was Whitton who forged the signature on the release papers, as Hamlet alleges?'

Alix shrugged her shoulders. 'Tying up loose ends?' Pausing, she added, 'It's something we need to look at, isn't it?'

'It is,' Jackson replied.

'But what about Thomas Midgley?' Lauren asked. 'What is the link between his murder and Tanya's? Both of these recordings have been sent through the app on Hamlet's phone, and the killer mentions Tanya and someone called Midge in the message. It would be fair to assume that Midge and Midgley are one and the same person; however, at this stage we haven't made a physical connection between the pair.'

'Nothing definite,' Alix confirmed. 'We have a photograph of him with a dark-haired girl, who we believe is Tanya when she was a teenager, but we haven't been able to confirm that yet. My guess would be that the link is the children's home, so I'm following that up tomorrow. I don't even know which children's home Tanya was in care at. As you know, she didn't tell her husband or her friend, Sally. I'm going to have to get a message to her brother in Afghanistan.'

'What about forensics at Midgley's home? Anything?' Jackson asked.

'Nothing yet, boss,' Alix replied. 'I spoke with Nate Fox half an hour ago. The forensics team had not long arrived. They were going to set things up and then leave and make an early start tomorrow morning. The pathologist has been, and Midgley's body has been bagged and removed to the Medico-

Legal Centre. Nate's going to secure the scene tonight and put a police guard on it.'

'Okay. Good.' Jackson looked at his watch and then at Lauren. 'It's too late now to start a briefing. I want everyone in for eight a.m. tomorrow. And I mean everyone. We're going to need two syndicates on this and we're going to have to include Derbyshire too. We've got Thomas Midgley's murder, Tanya Hodkin's death to upgrade to murder and we also have to review the murders of Helen Mottrell and Robert and Mary Mottrell, *plus* the death of Dr Whitton. My gut instinct is telling me that we have a real nutcase on the loose.'

A warm house greeted Alix as she opened her front door. After hearing the beep of her house alarm, she stepped into the hallway, pushed the door shut with her shoulder and punched in the code to deactivate the alarm.

Heaving out a gratifying sigh, she dumped down her bag and kicked off her shoes. It had been a long day and her feet were throbbing, but she couldn't relax yet. She had her karate lesson in an hour, and even though she was mentally exhausted it was the one thing she didn't miss, unless work prevented her. The two weekly sessions were the only time she could forget about the stress of her day job and get rid of any pent-up aggression. The kata at the end was especially relaxing, enabling her to re-focus her thoughts.

Putting on the deadbolt and double-checking the front door was secure, she shucked off her jacket and slung it over the stair banister before going through her coming-home ritual of checking each room. Only when she was happy that no one was lurking in any of the rooms did she undress and climb into the shower.

Washing away the day's grime under the warm jets, her thoughts were dominated by recent events. Her first serial-killer investigation and she was at the forefront of it. *Detective Sergeant Alix Rainbow. Who would have thought?*

Drying herself quickly and wrapping her damp hair in a towel, she fished out a pair of joggers and a T-shirt from her wardrobe and climbed into them. She was just starting to scrunch her hair dry when her mobile rang. Dropping the towel onto her bed she picked up her phone. It was her mum. *Shit!* She was supposed to be driving down to see her mother and father tomorrow. It had completely slipped from her mind.

Taking a deep breath and summoning up courage, she answered. 'Hi Mum, I was just going to call you.' She bit her bottom lip at the lie.

'About tomorrow?'

'Well, yes.' She took another deep breath. 'I'm afraid something's come up. I'm not going to be able to make tomorrow.'

'Oh Alix!'

'I'm sorry, Mum. An important case has just landed on my desk.'

'You said you'd come.'

'Yes, and I'm really sorry, but I honestly can't get away. It involves something that happened this morning. I can't say too much at the moment but you'll see it on the telly.' She never discussed work with her parents; she knew the worry it would cause them. The last thing she would tell her mum was that she was chasing a serial killer. Her mum would throw a fit. She added, 'You know I can't just drop things sometimes.'

'Even with your father seriously ill?'

Ouch! Alix breathed deeply. 'I'm really am sorry, Mum.' She paused. 'How is Dad?'

Her mother let out a long sigh. 'He seems okay. His faith keeps him going, as you know. He's not told any of his parishioners yet.'

'I will be down, Mum. Soon, I promise. I'll definitely make every effort to see him before he goes into hospital. Things should be sorted up here by then.'

'Your father will certainly appreciate you being here, Alix. We miss you. We haven't seen you for ages. I don't know, Alix, you always seem to put your work before us these days.'

Alix grimaced, tightening her grip on her mobile. 'Mum, that's unfair. Being a detective means I have so much work, especially with all the government cutbacks. I'm a sergeant now, remember, and that's only added to the pressure. You know that. I've told you.'

'I do remember. But you should remember that you only have one set of parents, Alix. You'll regret not having spent more time with us when we're no longer around.'

That's it Mother, pull the heartstrings tighter. 'Mum, I promise, as soon as things ease off, I'll be down. A week and things will be less hectic.'

'Okay. I'll phone this weekend to see how things are going.'

'Yes, that would be good. And tell Dad I'm thinking of him.'

'We'll say a prayer for you, Alix. Take care.'

The call ended. For a moment Alix stared at her phone. Then, in a flash of anger she threw it onto her bed, yelling at the top of voice, 'FUCK!'

Hamlet turned the Range Rover into the clearing and parked close to the cabin, where he sat for a moment steadying his breathing. He was still seething from Kieran Croft's headlines and his head was thumping from the stress. Stars were flaring behind his eyes. A migraine was starting. Soon he would be sick.

He gazed at his cabin and its surroundings, so grateful for this place. Its isolation meant no one could spy on him. He turned off the engine and hauled his shopping off the back seat, eyeing the two bottles of wine he'd bought. He'd take two paracetamol and then hopefully in a few hours he'd be able to open one of those to relax him. He needed a hit after the day he'd had. First up though was letting Lucky out for a toilet break. Then he'd put away his shopping and take the little terrier for a blast around the woods. The fresh air might help take the edge off his headache.

The moment he opened the door Lucky was waiting for him, mouth open and panting excitedly.

'Just a minute, boy. Let me put this lot down.' Hamlet carried the shopping bags into the kitchen and dumped them on the side, Lucky sticking close, almost glued to his legs. He pulled a carrot from a bag and held it out. Tail wagging as fast as a propeller, Lucky snatched it from his master's hand and went back to the kitchen doorway, where he dropped it and started to crunch.

Hamlet watched him gnawing through the carrot and broke into a smile. His tension was already easing. He had gone his whole life without a dog, never wanting one, declaring when Helen had wished for one that they wouldn't have time to look after one with their busy lifestyle. Finding Lucky had changed his whole perspective. Now, he was so grateful for the little dog's company.

Hamlet quickly put away the shopping, re-stocking cupboards and fridge and then took a long lingering look at the wine. It was early, he knew, but he really could do with a drink after the day he'd had.

He poured himself a decent glass, downed two paracetamols with his first swallow, and then made his way out onto the veranda, placing the glass on the table and pulling out a chair to slump into. Lucky followed him, giving his master a quick look, before scuttling off down the steps into the clearing where he cocked his leg against a tree.

Hamlet watched him for a couple of seconds, and then his gaze drifted toward the woodland beyond. The only sound was birdsong. So peaceful. He had always loved these woods.

He picked up his glass and took another mouthful of wine. As the mellow fruit notes filled his mouth, he instantly felt himself unwind. Taking another gulp, the visions of this morning visited him. It was the first time he had seen death like that. Sure, he'd seen far worse in movies, but this had not been the movies. What he had watched in those two recordings had been for real.

That thought suddenly took him back to the moment he'd woken up in hospital three years ago, when Detective Rainbow had leaned over his bed and told him he was being arrested for the murders of his wife and parents. The thought of what they must have gone through exploded inside his head. Had they been as frightened as he'd seen Tanya and Thomas when their moment had come? Hamlet shuddered, hoping not.

His eyes strayed beyond the glass he was holding to the long scar running along his forearm. His mind started to drift, transferring the images he had seen that morning to his own plight, visualising the knife ripping through his flesh. In his nightmares he could feel the knife tearing through his skin. But he was certain that it hadn't been a Stanley knife that had caused his wounds. Maybe he should go under hypnosis. See if he really could remember what happened. It might help him see who tried to kill him. Who murdered his beloved family.

Hamlet snapped his eyes shut. Part of him wanted to lock out the horrors, but a larger part wanted to remember.

ELEVEN

In the MIT briefing room, a large team of detectives were watching the recording of Tanya Hodkin's death. They had already sat through Thomas Midgley's murder.

DCI Jackson turned it off at the point of Tanya Hodkin's final moments.

Alix shuddered. She'd dropped her gaze the moment the Stanley knife started slicing into Tanya's arm. Now the recording had stopped, she lifted her eyes to face her DCI.

Jackson ran a hand over the top of his freshly shaved head. 'Okay guys, I think it would be fair to state we have a killer out there who we need to find fast. We know for certain, from what you've just seen, that this person has killed at least twice, but there is also the possibility that they are responsible for other murders, three of which we have previously investigated and one more which has been recorded as a suicide. And this is where I bring in Alix.' Jackson looked Alix's way, delivering a quick nod.

Alix eyed the two syndicate teams, her mouth forming into a soft smile. Clearing her throat, she said, 'Those recordings you've just seen were originally sent via a phone app to the mobile of a Dr Hamlet Mottrell.' She saw from their reaction that her colleagues recognised the name. 'As many of you know, Dr Mottrell was arrested for the murders of his wife and adopted parents three years ago, but was never charged on the instructions of the CPS, and was released. Last week, out of the blue, I was contacted by Dr Mottrell, who asked to speak with me about a death in Derbyshire. Myself and DI Simmerson went to speak with him at his home, where he showed us an article from a Derbyshire newspaper relating to the suicide of Tanya Hodkin. Dr Mottrell told us that not only did he believe Tanya's suicide was in fact murder, but that he knew who the murderer was.'

Alix went on to reveal Hamlet's story, first presenting Tanya Hodkin, *née* Johnson's background, and moving on to the children's home link with Hamlet's former patient, James Harry Benson, explaining that he had been a resident at the home when Tanya had reported him to the police for attempted rape back in 1995. Alix went on to disclose that Hamlet believed his former colleague, psychiatrist Dr Ian Whitton, had also been murdered — his death staged to look like suicide — and that the murders of Hamlet's family and his own near-fatal injuries had also been inflicted by the same person.

'The person that Hamlet believes carried out all these murders is James Harry Benson.' Alix paused at this stage, viewing the room. She could see that the majority were waiting for what she had to say next, but a few wore expressions of scepticism. *Typical detectives*, she thought, holding back a smile. Continuing, Alix detailed her follow-up enquiries, revealing the information DC Stones had provided about Tanya's evening out with her friend, the reaction to the drug she had taken that had been discarded by an unknown man in the bar, and the subsequent discovery of her body in the bath by her husband.

'DC Stones told me there was nothing to suggest that her death was anything other than suicide. The Stanley knife that had caused Tanya's injuries was on the floor beside the bath. There were no signs of a struggle and no signs of a break-in.' Pausing briefly, she added, 'I have to say, I had accepted that decision until I saw the recording yesterday.'

Alix went on to explain how, following their meeting at his home, Hamlet had received a text from a mysterious number with a link to a dark website, from which he had downloaded an app with instructions to contact her. She then told them about the document she had been sent by post of the image of the skull and what had happened when Hamlet had scanned it, leading them to the discovery of Thomas Midgley's body.

As she drew breath, a loud clap made Alix look up. All eyes turned to the podium where DCI Jackson had his hands clasped together. 'Thank you for that, Alix; very well briefed.'

She felt her cheeks flush.

'Okay, everyone,' Jackson continued, 'as you can probably imagine there is a lot of work to do here. First, we have the murder of Thomas Midgley. Schofield Street is our best crime scene, as it is the freshest and least compromised. Forensics will be starting there in the next hour. I want you, Alix, to go back there and take charge of the scene. I'll assign a team to you. See what you can find out from the neighbours about the victim and conduct a thorough search of the house.

'The recording suggests Tanya Hodkin and Thomas Midgley know one another. The man in the recording, our killer, calls him "Midge", so he definitely knows him. That is our best lead. I want to know everything about Thomas Midgley's past. See if we can confirm that he and Tanya knew one another from the children's home. See if we can find out what children's home that is. Let's start digging into Tanya's past before she was married. We know that in 1995 she made a complaint of attempted rape to the police. See if we can track down the officers who dealt with that.'

Jackson unclasped his hands and rubbed them together, throwing his team a determined look. 'We also need to go back to Tanya's home. It's over a month since her death, and the scene has probably been well and truly compromised by now, but we still need to do a thorough forensic examination. We might just get lucky. We'll have to move the husband out for a few days.

'I also want further lab tests on the blood sample from Tanya's post-mortem. Let's see if we can trace what that substance was that made her ill. And let's visit that pub she was in before she disappeared. See if it's got CCTV. Not just the pub, but the surrounding area as well. Tanya got home that night before she died. How? And was she helped by anyone?

'Go back to DC Stones. See if he's still got Tanya's phone. Get the Techs to go through it. DC Stones told us the mysterious text she was sent was from a pay-and-go. We need to have a fresh look at that. And we need to reinvestigate the suicide of Dr Ian Whitton. Again, we will need a thorough forensic examination of his home.

'Finally, we have the murders of Dr Mottrell's wife, Helen, and their unborn child, and his adopted parents, Robert and Mary. Dr Mottrell is not exactly off the hook, but there is the possibility now that someone else killed them and tried to frame him. On that note, I want the Techs to examine his phone and see if we can trace the IP address of the website where that app came from. I will be instigating a belt-and-braces review of his families' murders today.' Jackson took a deep breath, swelling his broad chest. Letting it out slowly, he said, 'I think we all saw last night's local paper. Not only is Dr Mottrell back in the headlines, but we are too. We need to go about our jobs professionally and keep tight-lipped on this. If this turns out to be the work of a serial killer, then we are certainly going to be under the spotlight.'

At her desk with her head down, Alix was filling in her daily journal, doing her best to ignore the chatter going on around her. It had been a very long day. She and Nate Fox had spent the best part of ten hours following the forensic team from one room to the next in Schofield Street, moving in to carry out a search the moment they moved out. All they had found by way of evidence was a stolen credit card, some counterfeit designer clothing, and a few wraps of cannabis bush. They had hoped to find more photographic evidence to link Thomas to Tanya, but that had proved fruitless and they now suspected that the photograph they had found of the teenage Thomas and the dark-haired girl had been brought to the scene by the killer.

They also hadn't found a phone for Midgley, and that made them suspect that the killer had taken it away with them. Alix had made a note to contact the main phone providers, but without a mobile number it wouldn't be an easy task.

House-to-house had not brought up anything of note; none of the neighbours had wanted to engage with the officers conducting that task.

The lack of progress had meant that the evening's briefing had been a frustrating affair. One success Alix had was learning the name of the detective who had dealt with Tanya's complaint of attempted rape back in 1995, though she hadn't had much success locating him. Detective Frank Mooney had retired almost eight years ago. His last job had been in the Intelligence Unit, the other side of Ecclesfield. When Alix had identified his name on the crime report in Tanya's case file, she instantly realised that she had heard of him, though had never met him. And when she had mentioned his name at briefing, several of the seasoned detectives of the syndicate said they knew him, two declaring that they had worked with him in the past, and she'd learned that Frank had been a well-liked and respected detective.

Before going into briefing she had run Mooney's name through the system but all trace of him had been wiped, leaving her with only one way of tracking him down — the police pensions department. Unfortunately, every number she tried had diverted to voicemail and it was quickly apparent to Alix that the department had shut down for the day, so after her fifth attempt she hung up, letting out a heavy sigh of frustration. Contacting them would be her first task tomorrow morning.

She looked up and saw that most of her colleagues were closing down their computers and slipping on their coats.

'Fancy a drink?' Nate called across to her, switching off his terminal.

Alix looked at her watch. Just after 9 p.m. She should really ring her mum to ask how her dad was, but after the day she'd just had the last thing she needed was her mum reminding her what a dutiful daughter would do given the nature of her father's illness. For a split-second guilt washed over her, but she quickly shrugged dit off. *I'll ring her tomorrow when I'm fresh. I'll be able to cope then.*

Alix rose from her seat. 'You've twisted my arm,' she replied, slipping her journal into her top drawer and locking it.

Swinging the axe high, Hamlet whipped it down, splitting the last log, imagining it was Kieran Croft's head. He smiled to himself. *I think that should see me through winter,* he thought to himself, looking at the pile of wood around him. He whacked the axe into a tree stump, leaving it looking like King Arthur's sword in its stone. He began collecting armfuls of split logs to stack neatly in his wood store at the side of the cabin.

Half an hour later, his chore finished, he ran his eyes over his winter fuel pile, feeling pleased with himself. When he had visited this place with Helen as their weekend retreat, chopping wood had been a fun thing to do before lighting an end-of-day fire for a romantic evening with a glass of wine. The thought conjured up an image of Helen snuggling into him in front of their log fire, the sound of the flames crackling in the grate as the pair of them made holiday plans. The memory led quickly to another. This one was of Helen with her golden hair tied back, wearing a summer dress, the front stretched tight over the swelling of her stomach, carrying the child he never got to see.

He wanted to hold on to the memory, but just as quickly as it had come it was gone again, leaving him with another, far, far darker. It was the image of Helen lying on their bed, dead, the duvet stained crimson around her. He hadn't seen her like that. The image, now burying itself into his brain, was a resurrection of events from three years ago, during his police interview. He had still been in a state of shock, after being told that Helen and his parents were dead, when Alix had pushed that crime-scene photograph of Helen's brutal ending across the desk, right under his nose, telling him to 'look at your handiwork.'

To be confronted with her death in that fashion had left him with constant nightmares. He knew why Alix had done it. He was the police's main suspect and they wanted a reaction from him. She had got a reaction all right. He'd erupted like a volcano, scattering the photo and paperwork across the interview room, screaming in horror before bursting into tears.

His duty solicitor had objected to her behaviour but the damage had been done. They had dragged him from the interview room and put him back in his cell to calm down. That episode had entered his thoughts many times over the past three years. Meeting Alix this week had revived that demon again. And, although he'd seen a different side to her, and his rational brain had told him that what she had done had been part of her job, he still couldn't truly forgive her. At some stage, she needed to know how he felt. He wanted her to know the mental anguish she had caused him. Only then would he feel his curse would be lifted. *First opportunity, I'm going to tell her.*

Tears suddenly welled up, blurring his vision and he squeezed his eyes shut to force them out. When he opened them again, Lucky was beside him, staring up, head to one side. Hamlet sensed the little dog felt his pain and wanted to comfort him. He bent down and ruffled his head, releasing a grin.

'Come on boy, shall we go for a walk?'

His tail wagging ferociously, Lucky spun around and bolted off in the direction of the stream.

This will clear my head, Hamlet told himself as he strode after him.

TWELVE

Following the morning briefing, Alix contacted the pensions department and got the telephone number for retired detective, Frank Mooney. She learned that he lived in Ringinglow, a small village on the edge of the Peak District moors. As she picked up the phone to call him, she felt a touch of envy. She had been to Ringinglow village pub — the Norfolk Arms — on numerous occasions to see folk bands and loved the location. It was the type of place she would aspire to retire to when her time came. Pushing away the thought, she tapped in Frank Mooney's number. He answered within two rings, his voice cautious, as if expecting it to be a cold-caller. After she introduced herself, he was less hesitant.

'What can I do you for, Sergeant Rainbow?' he said brightly.

Alix filled him in on recent events — the investigation into the murder of Thomas Midgley, and why they were exploring a link to Tanya — she referred to her by her maiden name, Johnson, the name he would have known her by — informing him that Tanya had been found dead with her wrists slashed and they were now treating her suicide as murder. She didn't tell him of the recordings they had received, but finished by saying that she had seen *his* name on the police system whilst digging into Tanya's past. She said, 'Do you remember that case, Frank?'

'Certainly do. I may have been out of the job a few years but I've still got a good memory.' He gave a light laugh. 'James Harry Benson was the boy involved, if my memory serves me right.'

'Spot on, Frank.'

'Tanya Johnson alleged that he'd tried to rape her. Me and my mate, Terry Palmer, he died last year, God bless him, got called to the children's home by care staff there. They'd locked Benson in his room following her allegation, but he'd set fire to the bedding and escaped out of the window. Uniform found him the next day, hiding out in woods not far from the home. He was wet through, close to hypothermia. Terry and I interviewed him after he'd been released from hospital. Big lad for his age and one weird kid, I can tell you. He didn't say a great deal, just stared across the table most of the time. Although, I have to say, I was never convinced he'd done what Tanya alleged.'

'What do you mean?'

'I know the police have taken a lot of stick for not dealing with sexual assault reports properly in the past, but this was one of those jobs that didn't smell right from the off.'

'You think she lied?'

'Couldn't prove it. I definitely think something went on between her and Benson in her room, but I wasn't convinced it was how she described things. Benson told us that she'd come on to him but when he couldn't get a hard-on, she'd started laughing at him, so he'd grabbed hold of her to try and shut her up. He was only charged because that mate of hers, Thomas Midgley, who you've just mentioned, backed up her story…'

Alix interrupted, 'Sorry to stop you there, Frank. Thomas Midgley? He was involved?'

'Yes. He was in the same children's home with Tanya and Benson. Thick as thieves with Tanya, apparently…'

Alix interjected again, 'You've just resolved the link between Thomas and Tanya. Thank you, Frank, that's made our job a lot easier.' Then, 'Sorry for interrupting. You were saying?'

'Yes. After we'd spoken with Tanya and Midgley we spoke to the care staff and they told us that there had been issues between Benson and Midgley. Midgley was known to be a bit of a bully and was 'Top Dog' at the home before Benson arrived. Midgley was a year older than Benson and staff told us that Midgley had tried it on when Benson first arrived, pushing his weight around, but Benson stood up to him and that caused a bit of friction between them. Then, roughly six months after Benson's arrival, Midgley was found semi-conscious in the toilets. His nose was broken. Midgley wouldn't say what had happened, but the care staff told us that the kids at the home had told them Benson had done it after Midgley had "offered him out".' Pausing, he added, 'If you want my opinion, Sergeant, I think Benson was set up. I think Tanya did instigate sex, but with a view to her then making a complaint of rape against Benson. And I think Midgley was the one who set it all up. That wasn't just my opinion. My partner was of the same view, as were the care staff. We interviewed Tanya three times, but she stuck to her story. As did Midgley, and Benson was charged. I think he got five years at court.'

'He did. Spot on again, Frank.'

He chuckled. 'See, nothing wrong with my memory.' Then, on a serious note, he said, 'I felt a bit sorry for Benson, actually.'

'Did you know he attacked a prisoner whilst he was in the young offender institution?'

'No, I didn't.'

'Yes, almost killed him. He alleged that the guy had tried to rape him in the showers, so he stoved his head in and told prison staff he'd heard voices in his head, telling him to do it. He was assessed by a psychiatrist and diagnosed with a personality disorder. They sent him to a secure unit, where he attacked another inmate. After that he was sent to Rampton Hospital, and then to Moor Lodge here in Sheffield, which he escaped from three years ago.' Alix went on to filled Frank in on Benson's escape from the medium secure unit.

'Bloody hell, that is some case you've got, Sergeant. I've not seen anything on the news or in the papers about Tanya or Midgley.'

'Until Thomas Midgley's murder, the day before yesterday, and the conversation we're now having, we hadn't joined up all the dots. You're the first person to link Tanya, Midgley and Benson together. You wouldn't remember the name of the children's home they were all in, would you?'

Frank Mooney was quiet. Then, he answered, 'Springfield. Springfield Children's Home, in Totley Brook. It's closed down now. It closed in early 2000.'

'That's a bummer. Well, at least it gives me a starting point to track down the staff who were there when Tanya, Midgley and Benson were. Just one more question, Frank, and then I'll let you go off to do whatever you do, now you're retired.'

He let out a hearty laugh. 'Not a lot at the moment actually. I've not long had a hip replacement. Still hobbling around. That's what you've got to look forward to when you retire, young lady.'

Alix laughed with him. Then, she said, 'The alleged attempted rape on Tanya? Was she examined at all?'

'Yes, we took her up to the Northern General with a member of the care staff. She was a bit reluctant, but we eventually managed to talk her round to being examined. They found no bruising to suggest she'd been molested.'

'That's helpful, thanks. I've tried to track down the prosecution file of the case, but it looks as though it's been shredded. The only details we have are recorded on the computer and they are really brief, so I'll try the hospital to see if they have any case notes for Tanya. I know it's a long time ago now but you wouldn't recall the name of the police surgeon who examined her, would you?'

There was another period of silence down the line. 'I believe it was a doctor who'd only just completed his training as a police surgeon. I remember chatting with him whilst I took his statement. His examination of Tanya was his first case. He told me he'd been training as a psychiatrist and had only just qualified and was applying for jobs. Now, what was his name?'

Alix was about to say that it didn't matter, when he blurted, 'Dr Whitton, I think his name was.'

'What? Dr Ian Whitton?'

'I can't remember what his first name was, but I remember it was Whitton, because Doug Whitton was our old collator, down in Crime Intelligence, and I asked him if he was related. Why, do you know the doctor?'

'Frank, you won't believe how helpful you've been.' She thanked him and hung up, adrenaline zipping through her like an electrical charge.

Alix looked at the notes she had made during her phone call. She would need to write a more comprehensive report for that evening's briefing. As she reached into her top drawer for her journal, her desk phone rang. She had only just announced her name when a man's voice said, 'I've just remembered something else.' It was Frank Mooney. 'It's about Benson.'

'Oh, yes?' Alix picked up her pen and grabbed a fresh piece of paper.

'It's about a girl who went missing from the home, shortly after Tanya made her allegation. And I think you'll find she's still on the National Missing Persons Database. I'm afraid I can't recall her name, this has only just come back to me, but you'll be able to chase it up, once I give you the circumstances.'

'Okay, go ahead.' Alix prepared to write.

'After Tanya had made her complaint, Benson was moved out of the home into another one. Still in the Sheffield area, but far enough away so he couldn't contact anyone. He moved schools as well, not that he ever bothered going, but then we found out he'd been in regular contact with one of the girls from Springfield.'

'Tell me more, Frank.'

'Uniform originally took the report.' He paused for a few seconds. 'I'm trying to wrack my brain for her name, but it just won't come. She had long dark hair. A year younger than Benson if I remember rightly.'

'It doesn't matter, Frank. As you say, if she's still missing, I should be able to trace her. She'll be on the system.'

'Well, as I say, uniform conducted the initial enquiries. It didn't come CID's way until she'd been missing for a week. Nothing slack in that. She'd gone missing from the home a few times before. She'd been found in an older guy's flat with a couple of other girls from the home. They were caught smoking joints. I think one of those girls might have been Tanya.

'Anyway, it was over the Christmas period, a couple of months after Benson had been moved, when she went missing. It was thought that she'd done the same as before — gone to stay at this guy's flat. Uniform visited him and searched his place — she wasn't there. They also interviewed him but he denied she'd been there. That's when the job came to us.

'I paid a repeat visit to the children's home and spoke with a couple of the kids there, including Tanya. At first, Tanya denied knowing anything, but I had a feeling she wasn't being honest with me and so I had a good go at her. That's when she told me that this girl had been going to Sheffield city centre on a regular basis and meeting up with Benson. On the day she went missing, Tanya said that the girl had confided in her that she was off to meet Benson to do some Christmas shopping.'

'What?'

'To be honest, Sergeant, and this is where I hold my hands up, I thought Tanya was trying to get Benson in trouble again, so I took what she told me with a pinch of salt, although I did go and question him.'

'What did he say?'

'Well, sure enough, he did admit that he'd met up with the girl on a few occasions since he'd been moved from Springfield but he denied she was his girlfriend. Just friends, he insisted. Nothing more. He told me that they had met up in McDonald's, near the cathedral, from time to time. But he denied having met her on the day she went missing. He said they had made plans to meet, and he went to McDonald's, but that she never turned up. He told us he'd mooched around the precinct, and gone down The Moor, and then back to McDonald's to see if she'd turned up. When there was no sign of her, he'd caught the bus back to the children's home he'd been moved to in Ecclesfield.

'The staff at the home confirmed he'd gone out mid-morning and that he was back for teatime. We did some follow-up enquiries at McDonald's, and in the city centre, but we drew a blank. No one could recall seeing the girl or Benson, but then again, that wasn't surprising. Firstly, over a week had gone by since she'd been reported missing, and secondly, they were just two teenagers among hundreds in Sheffield city centre the Saturday before Christmas.

'We concentrated a lot of our efforts on the older guy whose flat she and some of the other girls from Springfield had visited. I pulled him in and grilled him, but he stuck to the same story. Then, a few months after her disappearance, he was found dead from a drugs overdose. We had no other leads or enquiries to follow up and so the missing report was filed shortly after that.' Pausing briefly, he added, 'I wish now, especially after what you've told me, that I'd focussed more on Benson, but he was just a fifteen-year-old lad and he wasn't our main suspect.'

'You weren't to know at the time,' said Alix.

'Nevertheless, I should have looked at him closer. If I'm honest, not a great deal of energy was put into her disappearance. She was a kid in a children's home with a troubled background who regularly went missing.'

'I understand. It's done now. At least you've given me enough to re-examine her case.'

Suddenly, Frank exclaimed, 'Alice. Alice Crompton. It's just come back to me. She was fourteen.'

'Thank you, Frank. I'll make a few enquiries and then come back to you. I'll probably need a statement.'

As she hung up, Alix shivered.

THIRTEEN

The incident board in the Major Investigations Team unit had been split into three sections. The first section focussed on the murders of Thomas Midgley and Tanya Hodkin, their recent photographs side by side with a link-line drawn between them. Beneath each photo were their personal details and a timeline. Tanya's contained the most information, details transferred from her suicide report. Thomas Midgley's timeline was still under development.

Below that, several tasks had been listed. Two had question marks against them; the toxicology tests on Tanya's blood sample, and CCTV recordings from the pub and its surrounding area. The tests to determine which drugs were in Tanya's system at the time of her death were still being processed at the lab, and the designated CCTV viewing team were still watching through the hours of footage recorded during the evening prior to her death. It could be days before any results would be known.

The second section featured Dr Ian Whitton. As with Tanya's and Thomas's section anything of any value was scant. The total sum of everything they had about him came from the notes transferred from his suicide report from the coroner's file — there was a lot of work ahead, though a dotted line had been drawn linking him to Tanya because of the allegation of attempted rape she had made. They had to confirm it was Dr Whitton who had carried out her examination.

The third section focussed on the murders of Hamlet Mottrell's wife, Helen, their unborn child, and his adopted parents. Unlike the other two sections, this one was full of information and photographs. In large red lettering above selected crime scene photographs of each of the victims were the words UNDER REVIEW.

Taking centre stage above all of the sections was an A4 print-out of a photograph of James Harry Benson — his name in bold below it. It had been taken during his admission to Moor Lodge Secure Unit four years earlier. The unit had emailed it yesterday, letting them know Benson had grown a beard and his hair had been longer on the day of his escape. His features were quite striking, none more so than his boxer's nose and deep-set, dark eyes. He was six foot three and solidly built, which would make him stand out in any average crowd.

Next to the incident board was the interactive whiteboard. Projected upon it was a large head and shoulders photo of a caucasian, young-looking teenage girl, with a mane of long dark hair, centre parted.

DCI Jackson was on the podium. He brought evening briefing to order and, pointing to the incident board, said, 'Well guys, you can see that for the next few weeks, at least, we have a lot of work ahead of us. I've got a detective superintendent coming across from Rotherham tomorrow to review the Mottrells' murders. Whilst I don't believe we did anything wrong in that enquiry, seeing as, until these past few days, we didn't have anyone other than Hamlet Mottrell to focus our investigation on, the recent footage we've all seen of Tanya Hodkin's and Thomas Midgley's murders, together with the specific targeting of Dr Mottrell by someone who sent him the phone app, revealing how each of them died, has made us re-focus.

'That re-focus has also called into question the investigation into the death of Dr Ian Whitton, a former colleague of Dr Mottrell's, who we initially believed had committed suicide after being found responsible for forging Dr Mottrell's signature on James Harry Benson's day-release papers. There are now question marks in relation to his death.

'Okay then, tomorrow's work. I want everyone in for a seven a.m. start. We continue with the review of CCTV from the pub where Tanya was drinking on the evening before her death to see if we can find anything about this mysterious guy who supposedly dropped his drugs, which Tanya picked up and snorted in the toilets, believing it was cocaine. We know it wasn't cocaine, because there was none in her system, but we do know she snorted two lines of something, because her friend Sally witnessed it. We are still awaiting toxicology test results from Tanya's blood samples to see what that substance was, and although I've put in a phone call to hurry that along, it could be at least two more days before we have that result.

'In the meantime, now that we have a photo of James Harry Benson — although it's not a recent one — we should be able to see if he is our mystery man in the pub, or not. On the Thomas Midgley front, house-to-house hasn't brought anything of significance up. He was a known user of cannabis, and we have a bit of info about who provided him with his gear that needs following up, but other than that, zilch. His neighbours didn't see or hear anything untoward during the relevant times of his death. Or, so they say. They are both well known to us.' He grinned sarcastically. 'Forensics from his place will take weeks.

'Now, with regards to Tanya Hodkin. We now have the link between Tanya and Thomas Midgley that was bugging us yesterday. That link is Springfield Children's Home at Totley Brook, where they were both residents. That came to us courtesy of retired detective, Frank Mooney, who investigated Tanya's complaint of attempted rape against James Harry

Benson back in 1995. And of course we know that Benson was there at the same time. You'll get more on that background when Alix takes over.

'That brings me to the children's home. Frank Mooney tells us that he believes it closed in 2000.. As it was owned by the local authority, staff records and information on everyone who stayed there plus the daybook incidents should still be with the authority and so tracking them down is also a priority task. I'm mainly interested in the information recorded by staff of incidents involving Tanya, Midgley and Benson. I want as much background as possible about these three's years in that home. I'm convinced that period of time is key to Tanya and Midgley's deaths and that Benson is a person of interest over their killings.' Jackson cast his eyes over his audience. 'And on that note, I'll bring in Alix.'

Alix rose slowly from her seat, turning to face her colleagues. This was the part she hated most — performing centre stage. Drawing in a breath, she said, 'Before I talk about Tanya Hodkin and Thomas Midgley and give my reasons why we believe Dr Ian Whitton is now a possible murder victim, I want to introduce you to Alice Crompton.' Alix aimed a laser pointer at the interactive screen, drawing a red circle around the image of the dark-haired teenager. 'Alice was a resident at Springfield Children's Home at the same time as Tanya, Thomas and James Harry Benson. That was until the morning of the 23rd of December, the Saturday before Christmas, in 1995, when she was seen by a member of staff putting on her coat and walking out of the front door of the home.'

Alix let that sink in for several seconds before she added, 'That was the last time fourteen-year-old Alice was seen. She didn't come back to the home that day, or any other day thereafter. She simply disappeared.'

Alix went on to reveal the information Frank Mooney had given her, scanning faces as she talked. She could see she had their attention. Following Frank's call Alix had brought up the National Missing Persons Database and managed to track down an archived copy of Alice Crompton's missing-from-home report and photocopy it.

She finished by saying, 'Tanya Johnson, as she was known in 1995, was one of the last people to speak with Alice on the day of her disappearance, and she told Frank Mooney that Alice had told her that she was going in to Sheffield to do some Christmas shopping and to meet up with Benson. We can't prove or disprove whether Alice did go in to Sheffield because enquiries at that time didn't bring up any confirmed sightings of her after she left the children's home.

'We know that James Harry Benson, who was fifteen at the time, was interviewed initially by uniform, and also by Frank Mooney as a follow-up, and he admitted he did go into Sheffield with the intention of meeting up with Alice, but he claimed that she never turned up, and because of the lack of confirmed sightings of Alice we only have Benson's word for that.

'Information in Alice's missing-from-home report shows that a member of the care staff at Ecclesfield, where Benson had been moved following Tanya's complaint, confirmed he went out at around eleven-thirty a.m. on that Saturday and returned back just before five p.m., but we don't know what he did during that time. Given what we know, from everything that has gone on these past few days, it would be fair to state that Benson is now a person of significant interest in the disappearance of Alice Crompton as well.'

Alix returned her attention to the incident board. 'As you heard earlier, the boss has announced that we will be refocussing our attention on the suspected suicide of Dr Ian Whitton. I have already mentioned Dr Mottrell's suspicions regarding his death, but they are only suspicions. And to be honest, we don't actually have anything to prove or disprove whether those suspicions are founded or not. However, Frank Mooney revealed to me a very interesting piece of information this morning that certainly gives us another angle as to why we should re-open the case.'

With all eyes glued on her, Alix revealed that a Dr Whitton had been the police surgeon who had examined Tanya following her complaint. She judged from her colleagues' reaction that, like her, they had joined the dots.

This had just turned into a hunt for a serial killer.

FOURTEEN

Hamlet threw sticks for Lucky while repeatedly eyeing his watch as he waited for Detective Rainbow to arrive.

At just after 10 a.m. Alix's car finally appeared, churning up chunks of gravel as it swung off from the main road. As she drove towards him, he saw she was alone. *This is a first,* he thought, picking up Lucky and swinging open the gate for her to drive through. *It really must be informal, just like she said on the phone.*

She drove on for a few yards and came to a halt. Struggling with Lucky, who was squirming to get free, he pulled the gate shut, padlocked it and approached her idling car. Alix leaned across and sprung open the front passenger door. Hamlet had just put one foot inside when she stopped him, picking up her bag from the footwell and a folder from the passenger seat, before allowing him to climb in. His eyes followed the file which she dropped onto the back seat. It looked pretty thick, sheets of paper slipping out from between its blue cover, and he wondered if it contained information about the investigation. He tried to read some of the writing on the loose papers but couldn't get a clear view.

'Sorry I'm a bit late, Hamlet. I've just spent the last two hours with a retired detective who can talk the hind-leg off a donkey. I had to get a statement from him.'

He dragged his gaze away from the file to meet her dark brown eyes. 'You said you wanted to speak with me about Benson?' He studied her for a few seconds. The look she returned was not of someone who oozed confidence but someone who was suddenly vulnerable. He had seen this look many times, particularly when he had spoken with patients who had been victims, and he couldn't help but wonder why that was. The more he had seen of Alix Rainbow this past week the more he had become curious about her.

Alix gave him a small smile. 'Not that it's any consolation, Hamlet, but you'll be pleased to know that we've stepped up our interest in James Harry Benson. His name's just cropped up in relation to a girl who went missing from the children's home where he was a resident as a teenager. We've also made the link between Tanya and Thomas Midgley. They were also in the same children's home. That's why I'm late.'

'That's good news, but how can I help you in relation to this? I only got to know Benson four years ago.'

Alix set off driving slowly, the car rocking gently along the potholed track. 'That's why I want to have a chat with you. We want to know what he said during those sessions you had with him as his Responsible Clinician.'

'You can get all that information from Moor Lodge. All my reports will be on their system.'

'We're already on that. I emailed the request this morning, which I guess will take some time to be approved. In the meantime, my boss has sent me to see you in the hope you might be able throw light on where he's likely to be holed up. A place he's comfortable with or likely to gravitate to from his past.'

'I'm not sure I'll be able to help you there, but I'll try.'

Alix turned into the clearing and pulled up in front of the cabin, where she switched off the engine.

Hamlet opened the passenger door and released Lucky, who scampered off towards the veranda. Climbing out, he said, 'I'll make us a coffee and then you can fire away with your questions.'

Hamlet showed Alix into the cabin and made his way through to the kitchen where he put some fresh water in Lucky's bowl, filled up the kettle and made two coffees. Handing one mug to Alix, he said, 'Come on, let's go for a stroll while we talk. There's a place where we can sit and have a chat.'

Alix followed him outside and Hamlet led the way to the bench that overlooked the stream. It only took a couple of minutes to reach it, and as they approached he immediately saw that the detective was suitably impressed with the location. The stream rippled gently just below them, dappled sunlight dancing on the flowing water. On days like today Hamlet knew why his grandfather chose this spot to build their bench.

As if reading his thoughts, she said, 'Hamlet, this really is a beautiful place you have.'

As Hamlet sat down, a sadness suddenly overcame him. He answered, 'Yes, it is. But I'd rather it was still just a weekend retreat for me and Helen, like it used to be, instead of somewhere where I'm forced to hide. I would give anything to have those moments back.'

Alix offered a sympathetic look. 'I really am so sorry, Hamlet. I'm sorry for what we put you through.' She paused and added, 'For what *I* put you through. I only wish we had known what we know now.'

His eyes fixed on hers. 'But I tried to tell you, Alix. How many times did I say I didn't kill my family? You gave me such an horrendous time. You put me through the grinder when I should have been grieving.'

Alix nodded. 'I know, and I can only apologise again. The bottom line, though, is that James Harry Benson wasn't even on our radar. Three years ago, all the evidence we had pointed to you having killed your family, and then attempting to take your own life.'

Hamlet shrugged. He was hurting deeply, and yet at the same time, this conversation felt cathartic. For the first time it felt like he was being absolved of blame. 'I know, but the apology helps,' he said.

'You can help us catch the killer. Like you, I'm convinced Benson is at the heart of all this and you know so much more than us about him that may be of help. In fact, you're the *only* one at this moment. The others are dead.'

Releasing Alix's gaze, Hamlet took a sip of his coffee. 'How can I help?'

'Tell me about your discussions with Benson,' said Alix. 'You know the kind of things we're after. What makes him tick?'

Hamlet took a moment to reflect, his gaze drifting out across the stream. 'James Benson was one of the first patients I was introduced to at Moor Lodge. He was already one of Dr Whitton's patients when I arrived and so a good number of sessions had gone on between those two. Ian handed me his notes and asked me for my opinion. He said it was his view that James had achieved a great deal from the programme of treatment he had undergone, and it was his conclusion that he was no longer a danger to society. He thought he should be prepared for eventual release. Ian asked if he could assign him to me for my opinion and I agreed to take him on.'

Hamlet paused. 'The first thing I always do is read a patient's notes before I engage in any session with them. Benson's notes surprised me. They lacked detail. They told me very little about him as a person or what had made him become the person who had viciously attacked several people. Psychology is all about understanding people's motivation, what makes them do the things they do and, with Benson, there was nothing in those notes that helped me form a structured picture of his personality. Sure, they gave me a little about his family background and his crimes, and they told me that in Rampton he had successfully followed various courses in social skills training, victim awareness, and anger control, and he'd also participated in occupational therapies. But that was all. His notes were extremely weak, and so I decided that the first thing I would do is build up a rapport with him and take him right back to the beginning of his early life and memories.

'It would be fair to say that from the off, Benson was very elusive. Don't get me wrong, he was polite, made all the right noises of compliance, "yes sir, no sir", but it was my impression this was a show by him. At first he resisted and I had to threaten him with sanctions. No computer- or art-classes. You wouldn't believe how something so simple has such an amazing power of persuasion in prison environment. Once he'd missed a few classes he agreed to participate, but it took a long time for him to respond to my questions.

'We started by talking about his early years. As I say, I had read his file, but I wanted to check if there was any deviation from what he had told others. I began by asking him to talk about his parents. His immediate answer was to tell me that both his parents were dead and he was orphaned when he was eleven. Now, whilst this was true, I happened to know from his notes that both his parents were in fact killed.'

'Killed?'

'I don't know the precise circumstances. Only the scantest of details were in his file. It was a case of murder-suicide: his father had killed his mother and then taken his own life. When I probed Benson on this, he said he didn't want to talk about it, that his father was a drunken bully whose death was no sad loss. I tried to talk to him about his schooldays and early family life, but he skirted around them.

'Several times I brought up the relationship he had with his parents and he shut up shop. In fact, he got angry in one of our early sessions, so I decided to leave it until I had built up a relationship with him.' Hamlet saw that Alix had her journal out and was making notes. 'We touched on what happened after he became an orphan, and he told me he had been sent to several foster parents, but he just never got on with them and so ended up in a home.'

'What about his extended family? Grandparents? Other relatives?'

'I asked him about that and he said he hardly knew any of his relations because of what his dad was like, and that nobody in the family had come forward, which was why he went to those foster homes.'

'Gosh, that's sad.'

'Isn't it? I did ask him on several occasions what he felt about that and he just shrugged his shoulders. I wasn't surprised by that reaction. I could see he was putting up barriers so I couldn't get inside his head. I did determine, however, that he displayed a complete lack of empathy, which is often associated with sociopathy and psychopathy.'

'Hamlet, did you talk with him about what went on at the children's home in Totley Brook?'

'I did, because obviously that was the first time he came to any of the authorities' notice. We covered it over a couple of sessions. It was the only time he opened up to me. He told me about the allegation Tanya had made and continually denied her version of events. He said she'd made it all up. I went over the circumstances of the allegation with him, because some patients disassociate themselves from their crimes. I wanted to see if I could get him to change his story. However, James never deviated from his denial. He stuck to his account that Tanya had made the whole thing up.'

Alix stopped writing and looked up. 'That's interesting because I spoke with the detective who dealt with the case and he told me that he got the feeling that Tanya wasn't telling the truth about the allegation she made against Benson, and that one of the reasons he was charged was because it was corroborated by Thomas Midgley.'

'Midgley?'

'Yes, Thomas Midgley was in Springfield at the same time. The detective — he's retired now — confirmed that for us. Apparently, he and Benson didn't get on. Midgley was a bit of a bully, and he and Benson had a set-to one day and Midgley ended up with a broken nose. It's therefore a possibility that Midgley and Tanya set Benson up. Did he ever mention Midgley?'

Hamlet shook his head. 'No, he only mentioned Tanya.' He paused, then added, 'Well, that would certainly give Benson, in his disturbed mind, a motive for killing both Tanya and Thomas Midgley.'

Alix nodded. 'That's what we're now looking at. And the detective also told me that it was a Dr Whitton who examined Tanya at the hospital after she made her allegation, and his assessment would have been part of the prosecution case. We've got to check and confirm that it was the same Dr Whitton, though we're sure it is. It would appear that he was working as a police surgeon following his qualification as a psychiatrist.'

'Wow, so that's a clear connection between Dr Whitton and James Harry Benson, prior to Benson's admission to Moor Lodge.'

Alix nodded.

'So, if it was Ian, he should have disclosed that during his sessions with Benson.' Hamlet frowned. 'I don't remember seeing it on Benson's file.'

'There's the possibility that Ian wouldn't have made the connection. Benson was only fifteen when he was convicted. And it was nineteen years before Ian came into contact with him again at Moor Lodge. He might not have recognised Benson, or made the connection because of the time lapse.'

'If that's right, and Benson realised who Dr Whitton was, then that could mean Benson killed him out of revenge for giving that statement to the police back in 1995? Thoughts of revenge can simmer for a long time before boiling over and this has been in Benson's psyche since he was fifteen. There would have been a lot of pent-up anger inside him so it is feasible as a motive.'

Alix shrugged her shoulders. 'It certainly is a theory that will need to be explored. We've only just re-opened the investigation into Dr Whitton's death, and it's not going to be easy. That's why I'm here, to see if you can throw any light on it.'

Over the next hour Alix fired questions at Hamlet which he answered, though he could tell from the number of sighs she released that he wasn't providing the responses she was hoping for. He explained that without his notes to refer to, he knew nothing much more of his past than she did, and he definitely couldn't recall him ever mentioning anyone that he was close to, or fond of.

'James Harry Benson was a loner,' he told her. 'He engaged only where he had to, and even then, he didn't reveal much.' Hamlet took a sip of his coffee, grimacing as a cold bitterness filled his mouth. He glanced across at Alix's mug and guessed hers would be cold too. 'Shall I get us another?' he said, throwing the dregs into the soil. She nodded and handed her mug over. He slung the cold remains in the direction of the stream and returned to the cabin where he made a fresh brew.

When Hamlet returned, Alix was standing on top of the bank, looking down over the stream.

She turned as he set down the mugs. 'You really have got a stunning place here, Hamlet. I would give my right arm to live somewhere like this.'

'You wouldn't say that in winter. Not that it's exactly freezing because I've got my log fire, but it can be pretty gloomy and certainly lonely if we get a heavy fall of snow.'

'I bet it was fun as a kid. You did say you used to come here with your grandfather on a regular basis, didn't you?' she said, returning to the bench.

'Most weekends. I certainly spent most of the school holidays here.'

'Did your parents come here much?'

'They did, but it was only usually for the odd day — barbeques and the like. This was mine and Grandad's place. We spent a lot of time here. As you know my adoptive dad was a doctor, so he always seemed to be out working, and Mum was always busy with charity stuff from what I remember, so weekends and holidays I came here with Grandad.' Hamlet looked at Alix and could tell she was asking out of interest rather than probing as a detective. 'Don't read anything untoward in that. The time I did spend with my adoptive parents was quality. They gave me so much support, especially helping me qualify as a doctor myself.' He let out a light laugh. 'You're making me sound defensive.'

Alix laughed with him. She picked up the fresh coffee he'd made, took a drink and gazed out across the stream again. Hamlet was suddenly conscious of a light wind that had picked up whilst they had been sat there. It was gently swishing the top boughs of the trees, though it wasn't cold by any means. *Actually, quite pleasant, just sat here*, he thought. He hadn't had a decent conversation with another adult for years.

'What about your real parents, Hamlet?'

'Never knew them. By that, I mean I can't remember them. They died in an accident when I was two and a half and that's when I was adopted.'

'What about any extended family?'

Hamlet shrugged. 'No idea. To be honest, in my early twenties I did think about seeing if I could trace my family, but then I felt as though I would be betraying the mum and dad who had brought me up and loved me. It didn't seem right, so I never bothered.'

'What was your birth surname?'

He threw another shrug. 'Don't know. My adoptive parents changed my surname by deed poll and I've never seen my birth certificate. I never asked for it. That might sound strange but once I'd made the decision not to bother tracing my family, it never interested me to find out. I'm so grateful for the time my adoptive family gave me. I suppose that's why it's hurt and affected me so much, not just the fact that they've been murdered, but that you blamed me for their deaths.'

Alix turned to him, a guilty and sorrowful look plastered on her face. 'Yes, I guess so. I can see that now. I'm sorry.'

Hamlet acknowledged her apology with a small smile and changed the subject by asking, 'What about your parents? I think you said your dad was a vicar?'

She instantly spun her face away from him and started rubbing the inside of her right thigh.

Hamlet knew he had uncovered something that disturbed her deeply. He had sensed it before and her reaction this time confirmed he was on to something. But what?

Alix slowly turned. In the short time she had been looking away her eyes had welled up. 'Things are a little strained between me and my dad,' she answered, biting down on her bottom lip.

Hamlet studied her for a moment before gently saying, 'Do you want to talk about it?'

Blinking, a solitary tear trickled down her left cheek to the corner of her mouth. She sucked it in. 'I was raped.'

Her response was not what Hamlet had expected. He was about to ask if she wanted to discuss it when Alix's phone started ringing. He inwardly cursed, wanting to tell her to ignore it, but she reached into her jacket and pulled it out, brushing away the tear streak as she viewed the screen. 'It's my DI,' she said, without looking his way. 'I need to get this.'

Although Hamlet listened in he couldn't make sense of the conversation because Alix was doing a lot of listening, answering with the occasional 'What?' and 'Never!' It was obvious, however, that something pretty serious was being said on the other end of the line.

Finally, she said into the phone, 'I'll get over there straight away. It'll probably take me about forty minutes.'

'Something happened?' Hamlet asked, as Alix ended the call.

'I'm needed urgently. And I need you to come with me. I'll explain on the way.'

FIFTEEN

Hamlet gripped the edge of his seat, a mixture of excitement and terror coursing through him as yet another driver blared their horn as Alix made a hair-raising overtake. They were racing up to Ringinglow following DI Simmons' phone call telling her that Frank Mooney's body had just been found by his wife and that it looked like he'd killed himself.

The moment Hamlet had jumped into Alix's car she had turned on her police radio, and they had listened in as Alix sped along the motorway. From the frequent updates, he learned that the retired detective had been found in his home with his wrists slashed and that he was already dead when paramedics responded to his wife's emergency call half an hour ago. Members of Alix's team had also been dispatched and Hamlet gathered from the radio chatter that they were almost on the scene.

Alix took her foot off the accelerator, braking as they entered the village, dropping from 60mph to 30mph in a matter of seconds. Hamlet hadn't been here before, and as they passed the first few stone houses with large slate roofs, he could only reflect on how beautiful the place was. In the bright autumn sunshine the stone lit up the colour of honey, adding to the picturesque value of the village. Behind the houses, he saw that gardens backed onto a vast expanse of open countryside leading out to the moors of the Peak District, and whilst at this time of year the place looked beautiful, he could guess that it would be pretty bleak during the winter. *A bit like my place*, he thought.

A hundred yards ahead, Hamlet spotted a cluster of haphazardly parked vehicles, among them an ambulance with its roof-lights flashing, clearly earmarking that they had reached their destination. Alix started pulling in, tucking in behind the last parked vehicle and came to a halt. A few yards ahead, to Hamlet's left, was a derelict low stone building that reminded him of an ancient chapel and beyond that, jutting out onto a grass verge, was an octagon-shaped house that looked as though it had once been an old toll house. Ahead, the road led to a junction, where, on the opposite side, was a large stone coaching inn signposted as the Norfolk Arms.

Alix pointed out through the windscreen, 'Frank's cottage is through the gate, next to the Roundhouse.'

Hamlet saw she was pointing to the octagon building. 'What do you want me to do?' he asked.

'Just hang on here for now whilst I go and see what the situation is. Given that I only saw Frank this morning for a statement, there's something not right. You've already gathered from the radio transmissions that Frank's been found with his wrists slashed. Alarm bells are telling me that we might have a similar situation to the one with Thomas Midgley.'

'That can mean only one thing.'

'I'm already on the same wavelength as you, Hamlet. It's been running through my mind all the way here. It probably means that Benson followed me here this morning. And, if that is the case, then it's pretty damn scary — it means we're up against a calculating and dangerous individual.'

'He could be watching us right now.' Hamlet scoured the road up ahead where a group of people had clustered, seeing if he could pick out anyone who looked remotely like James Harry Benson, but it was proving difficult to get a clear view because of the haphazard parking of the emergency vehicles.

'As soon as I'm kitted up my priority is to get uniform to check everyone in the immediate location.' Alix removed the ignition keys and opened the car door.

As she climbed into her disposable forensic suit, Hamlet's eyes drifted around, a slight edge of apprehension creeping over him. *Was Benson still here?* As his eyes settled back on Alix, looking more like an astronaut than a detective, his stomach flipped and he felt sick. He couldn't help but wonder if the killer was close by, watching.

After Alix had disappeared through the gate that led towards Frank Mooney's cottage, Hamlet remained in the car watching the small crowd that had gathered, scrutinising each face to see if any of them reminded him of Benson. Thankfully, none did and the knot in his stomach started to untie itself. Twenty minutes later, Alix reappeared, pulling down her facemask. As she walked towards him, Hamlet couldn't help but think how professional and in control she looked, given what he now knew about her. While she had been in the Mooneys' home he had given some thought to her revelation earlier: he had been right to think she was hiding something.

Alix opened the car door to get in and a cold blast of air caught Hamlet by surprise. He had been sat behind glass since they'd arrived, being warmed by bright sunshine for the last twenty minutes, not realising how chilly it was up here on the edge of the moors.

'It's almost the same scenario as Midgley,' Alix told him now. 'Frank's sat in his armchair with his wrists slashed. There's a bump and a small gash to his head, so it looks as if he could have been knocked unconscious prior to the offender cutting his wrists. There's no weapon at the scene and we've got the pathologist and forensic team on their way. We're just about to seal the place off, but before that happens I need to show you something. The killer has left us another message.'

'You need me to come in with you?'

'Yes. You'll need to put on a suit though. I've got a spare one in the boot, and when we get to the cottage stay as close as you can to me.'

Alix helped Hamlet into the forensic suit, letting him lean on her as he slipped it on. Then the two of them strode towards Frank Mooney's cottage, the forensic onesies rustling with every step.

As Hamlet neared the stone cottage, he gave it the once over. It had a lower and upper storey, four leaded mullioned windows painted cream, and a varnished wooden door. His initial thought was *quaint*. As he followed Alix up the path to the front door, he noted that the garden was well maintained, with many of its flowers still in bloom even though the end of September was looming.

A police officer in high-vis was guarding the open door. She held a clipboard and as they approached she started scribbling something down.

'This is Dr Hamlet Mottrell,' Alix said, as she stepped past her and into the hallway.

As Hamlet passed the officer, she scrutinised him and his immediate thought was *I bet she's wondering what I'm doing here?* He gave her his best friendly smile but it went unreturned.

'Pull your mask up, Hamlet,' Alix told him, looking back over her shoulder.

Following her instructions, he pulled up his facemask and followed her into a narrow hallway that was no more than four yards long. A door was open at the other end and he spied the kitchen beyond. To his right, just before the kitchen door, was another open doorway, through which sunlight poured into the hall. The light settled on a small dark stain by the entranceway and he caught Alix's attention, dipping his head in its direction.

'We think that's where Frank was first hit,' Alix told him. 'I'm guessing that his attacker was probably hiding behind the door.His wife has told us that she left to go shopping just after half-nine this morning, after I'd left them to drive to yours, and that when she left, Frank was getting ready to go out for a stroll. He was going to go up to the reservoir at Redmires, which is about a mile and half from here. He's not long had a hip replacement and he's been doing steady exercise.'

Hamlet nodded.

'We've discovered that the kitchen door has been forced, so what we're running with at the moment is that Frank's come home from his walk, and whoever broke into the house took him by surprise; clobbered him with something, rendering him unconscious, and then dragged him into the lounge, plonked him in the armchair and then … well, you can guess the rest. Frank's a big guy, but there's no sign of a struggle. I can't imagine Frank not putting up some kind of a fight if he'd have been conscious.'

Nodding again, Hamlet responded, 'Benson would be bigger, stronger and younger than Frank.'

Alix stood by the door into the lounge, avoiding the stain on the floor, indicating with her head for him to go inside.

As soon as he stepped into the doorway, Hamlet saw the scene Alix had described. The retired detective was slumped in an armchair, his head dropped to his chest. His arms were resting on the sides of the chair, his wrists and hands coated in dark crimson blood. More blood had cascaded over the sides of the chair and pooled on the beige carpet. His eyes were shut.

Hamlet could see a small gash to the right side of his forehead, just below his hairline. The scene was similar to the one that had faced him at Schofield Street, though whereas Thomas Midgley had been placed on a straight-back chair, Frank Mooney was in a comfortable armchair. What he couldn't miss was the message daubed on the wall above the fireplace, which immediately cemented in his mind the belief that the same killer was responsible. It was the same missive as before, though this time it looked as if it had been painted with Frank's blood. #YouCan'tHide stretched across the chimney breast and the letters were at least a foot high. Below that, and in smaller lettering, was scribed 'Seek, and ye shall find.' Some of the blood had run down the wallpaper.

The killer is definitely making a statement this time.

'That's what I needed you to see,' said Alix.

Hamlet stared at the sentence that he now knew off by heart.

'Before CSI get here can you see if anything comes up on your phone?'

Hamlet fished awkwardly around in his forensic suit, finally pulling out his mobile from his trouser pocket and keying in his password. He enabled the mysterious app he'd been sent and watched the juggling balls pulsate for a few seconds before forming into a circle, then he aimed it at the wall, adjusting his position to capture the whole sentence.

Suddenly the screen flickered, conjuring up an outdoor grassed setting with grey stones poking out of the ground. The video was shot from a low angle with just a flash of sky showing at the top of the screen.

Hamlet could feel Alix's breath on his neck as she peered over his shoulder. The shaky picture stilled, fixing onto one of the grey stones. As the image became more defined Hamlet realised he was looking at a headstone in a graveyard. He started to read the carved inscription as it slowly became clearer, but before he could finish reading it a slip of coloured paper appeared on screen, obscuring the engraving. It was a photograph of a dark-haired teenage girl. It floated around the screen for a couple of seconds before disappearing, as if by magic, into the grave. Then the picture faded to black.

'I recognise that photograph. That's Alice Crompton,' gasped Alix.

'Who's Alice Crompton?' Hamlet asked, lifting his eyes from the screen.

'A girl who went missing just before Christmas in 1995. She was in the same children's home as Tanya, Thomas and James Benson.'

SIXTEEN

The MIT team were gathered in the briefing room, among them two senior detectives from Rotherham, who had come to review the Mottrell murders. Most eyes were focussed on the whiteboard: the latest addition to the storyboard was the murder of Frank Mooney, a photo of the former detective dead in his armchair, and next to it a shot of the words '#YouCan'tHide' and 'Seek, and ye shall find' daubed across the chimney breast in Frank's blood.

DCI Jackson was standing beside the board, mouth set tight, his gaze bouncing from one seated member of his team to another. He cleared his throat loudly, bringing the room to order. 'Good evening everyone. I think it would be fair to say it's been a long day, and I don't know about any of you, but I for one hear the pub beckoning.' His mouth cracked into a grin and then he clapped his hands together. 'And on that note let's open things up. Alix, tell us what we've got.'

Alix shuffled in her seat, shot a quick glance at her journal to reassure herself and said, 'I've been at Frank Mooney's place all of this afternoon, right up until an hour ago, and I don't think I'm speaking out of turn here when I say his death bears all the hallmarks of Thomas Midgley's murder. There are many similarities that tell me the same person killed both Frank and Thomas.

'For instance, both victims have been placed in a chair and had their wrists slashed with a sharp instrument. And then there's the same message left for us to find, which links to the app on Dr Hamlet Mottrell's phone — I'll come back to that in a minute.

'There are, however, a couple of small differences. In the case of Frank's murder, the killer didn't just let themselves into the house, like in the case of Thomas Midgley, who we know regularly left his door unlocked. In Frank's case he was out this morning, walking, and Mrs Mooney was out shopping and so the house was locked up. The house is on alarm but Frank's wife told us she doesn't always set it, and this morning she was expecting Frank to be home not long after she left so she didn't bother setting it.

'Whoever killed Frank broke into the house by forcing the rear kitchen door and then most probably lay in wait for him to come home. It appears, from a small cut and bump to his forehead, that Frank had been caught by surprise by his attacker and more than likely rendered unconscious by a blow to his head. CSI have also found a minute amount of blood to the right-hand side of his neck caused by a puncture wound. The pathologist has examined this injury and believes it to have been caused by a hypodermic needle. It looks as though Frank was injected with something. A blood toxicology screen at the post-mortem tomorrow afternoon will reveal more.

'If the substance injected was one which incapacitated him, then it will explain why Frank did not resist, or put up a fight.' Alix paused. She could feel her hand trembling slightly. 'That's not all that concerns me about Frank's murder. His death happened not long after I visited him this morning. It's my belief that I inadvertently let our killer know where Frank lived. I'd arranged to see him this morning to get a statement in relation to the Thomas Midgley and Tanya Hodkin investigations, which leads me to believe that I was followed to his house by his killer.' She took a deep breath. 'Ringinglow is a remote village. It's not a place you would drive through to get anywhere. Not only is the village remote but so is the location of Frank's cottage. It's tucked away off the main road, hidden behind the old toll house. I can't imagine for one minute that whoever killed him has come across his cottage by accident.'

Alix reminded the team of Frank's investigation into Tanya's allegation of attempted rape against James Harry Benson back in 1995, and also Thomas Midgley's role in supporting her claim. Then she said, 'With regards to that information, I went to his house at around eight-thirty this morning and took a statement from him, and as I was leaving, Mrs Mooney was just getting ready to go out to do some shopping and Frank told me that he was going off for a stroll to Redmires reservoir. He's recently had a hip replacement operation and he's been building up his exercise regime. After I left their cottage, I drove straight over to Dr Mottrell's place to speak with him about James Harry Benson. I was at his place when I got the call about Frank.'

Katie Turner, seated behind, asked, 'You said that you believe Frank's killer followed you to his house. Did you actually notice anyone following you, Alix?'

Alix shook her head. 'To be honest, Katie, I didn't. But then, that was the last thing on my mind. I'd fixed up to take a statement from him, and was focussed on the background I needed to get on that, and I was also thinking about my meeting with Dr Mottrell. Although I looked in my rear-view mirror while I was driving, I didn't really take much notice of what particular vehicle was behind me.'

Jackson interjected, 'Don't beat yourself up, Alix. I don't think anyone in this room is blaming you for what happened to Frank. And, I don't think for one minute any of us would have anticipated the killer to be following detectives involved in the investigation. It would be a first for me if that is the case.' He paused momentarily and added, 'And, to be honest, Alix, we don't know for definite that is the case. It could well be that this is a pure coincidence. I hear what you're saying about the remote location of Frank's cottage, but if Benson is our killer, he's already spent time and effort tracking down the whereabouts of Tanya, Thomas, and Dr Whitton since his escape from Moor Lodge. Frank Mooney would be another on his list, if his motive is revenge, because it was *his* investigation that got him jailed. It's not exactly hard these days to trace people if you know where to look.

'But this is a wake-up call everyone. If Alix was followed by our killer, I want everyone from now on to be on their guard. If you suspect that you are being followed, you call it in and get back-up, soon as. I don't want any heroics. And on that note, I'll hand the briefing back to Alix.'

With a half-smile Alix responded, 'Thanks, Boss.' Then, composing herself, she continued. 'Once I got the call from DI Simmerson, I decided to go straight to Frank's place with Dr Mottrell, because I had a feeling our killer had struck again and the app on Dr Mottrell's phone might be needed, and I was right. As you can see from the photo on the incident board, our killer has left us another message. This one, above Frank's fireplace, looks as though it's been written in Frank's own blood. Before I show you what the result was using the app on Dr Mottrell's mobile, I'll give you a quick run-down of what we currently know about Frank's murder.'

Alix glanced again at her notes. 'I left around nine-thirty, and Mrs Mooney left shortly before Frank set off on his walk. She returned home about two-thirty. She told us the front door was open, and that she went into the hallway, could see through to the kitchen that the back door was open but didn't realise it had been forced and shouted through to her husband.

'When he didn't answer, she walked along the hallway to the lounge and saw him through the open door, slumped in the armchair exactly like you see in the crime scene photograph. As soon as she saw the blood, she ran straight back out of the house to her neighbours at the Roundhouse, where she rang for the police. We have that call recorded.

'And that's where I come into it. Dr Mottrell and I reached the cottage at just after quarter past three. As soon as I saw the message above the fireplace, I got Dr Mottrell suited up and inside the cottage to use the app on his phone. This is what was recorded.'

The large interactive screen at the front of the room lit up and the footage downloaded from Hamlet's mobile began playing. They ran through the recording once for the team to digest, and then DCI Jackson said, 'I'm going to play this again. Only this time I'm going to freeze it at the moment just before the photograph floats in front of the headstone, which is where Alix is going to come back in.' Pausing, he added, 'Except for our Rotherham guests, does everyone recognise the girl in the photograph?'

Almost everyone in the room nodded.

'It's Alice Crompton, who was reported missing two days before Christmas in 1995, after supposedly leaving Totley Brook Children's Home to meet James Harry Benson.' Jackson set the recoding going again. Ten seconds in, he froze the footage as the headstone came into focus and the inscription could be clearly read. The headstone had the name Elsie Davenport inscribed upon it. Elsie had been eighty-two years old when she had died, and the date of her death was inscribed as the 10th December 1995. Jackson looked directly at Alix. 'I believe you've already made some enquiries into Elsie's death?'

Alix nodded. 'As you can see, Elsie Davenport died on the 10th of December 1995. She died in Northern General Hospital, from pneumonia, so there is nothing suspicious about her death. I haven't yet been able to check if Elsie is related to any of our victims, or to Alice Crompton, but if my thinking is correct then I don't believe she is related to anyone involved in this investigation. Elsie's grave has been chosen purely because of circumstances.'

'You've already shared your thoughts with me, Alix. Will you now share them with the team?' said Jackson.

'Yes, Boss.' Alix shifted to face her colleagues. 'Every message left by our killer has given us clues to something that has happened. First, the dramatic announcement of the death of Thomas Midgley from the skull photograph sent to me. Then, when we found Thomas's body at his house, the true cause of Tanya Hodkin's death was revealed by the message left with his body. And now we have this video, following Frank Mooney's murder, which links us to Alice Crompton, a girl who was known by both Thomas and Tanya, and who herself has been missing since 1995. Frank spent a short time investigating her disappearance, but it was believed to be linked to an older man she used to visit to smoke weed with and nothing to do with Benson.' Alix turned and pointed towards the screen where the image of Elsie Davenport's headstone was frozen. 'Although we can all see from the inscription that Elsie died on the 10th of December, in 1995, she wouldn't have been buried on that day. It would have been later, probably around the time Alice went missing. I've yet to find out where the churchyard where Elsie is buried is, or the exact date she was buried, but I believe that the killer is telling us that Alice Crompton is buried in Elsie's grave.'

SEVENTEEN

After waving goodbye to Alix, Hamlet made his way slowly up the track to the cabin. Halfway along, for no apparent reason, he started to shake, quickly followed by uncontrollable sobs, forcing him to stop. He knew what it was. Shock. The sight of Frank Mooney's body in the armchair, blood pooled around him from his slashed wrists, had triggered the attack. It brought back the events of three years ago all over again.

These past few days had brought him hope. But the sight of the dead detective had brought everything back. As if the killer hadn't punished him enough by murdering his entire family, now he was making him suffer again thanks to that app he'd been sent. This was the killer's payback to everyone he believed to have wronged him.

Hamlet firmly believe that his punishment was because he had been instrumental in making the recommendation for Benson to be returned to prison because he had determined that he still posed a danger to society. And, if the killer was indeed Benson, then he had been proved right. Hamlet had been wrestling, however, with why he had killed Dr Ian Whitton. Even if he had given a statement back in 1995 following his examination of Tanya Hodkin, Whitton had more than made up for it by forging Hamlet's signature on Benson's day-release papers. Hamlet struggled to understand why Whitton had done that, surely knowing how dangerous Benson was. And the forgery was against professional practice. When he had first learned of Whitton's death three years ago, he'd believed, like the police, that he had died by suicide.

But now that Alix and her team were reinvestigating his death, Hamlet couldn't understand why Benson would want to kill Ian.

As he entered the clearing to his cabin, Lucky bounded down the steps of the veranda and bolted towards him, tail wagging. The dog instantly lifted Hamlet's spirits and he scooped him up and let him lick his face. 'And I'm pleased to see you, as well,' Hamlet greeted him, nuzzling his ears. Releasing him, he watched him scamper back to the veranda. 'Let's get you some food, young man,' he called. 'You must be starving. I know am.'

He opened the door and let Lucky inside. His dog made straight for the kitchen and Hamlet followed, picking up his bowl. He filled it with some dried food, and opened up a small tin of pilchards from the cupboard, stirring them together as a treat. Lucky attacked the dish the moment Hamlet set it down. Then, he went about getting his own meal, selecting a meal-for-one from the freezer and popping it in the oven. As a side dish he emptied a tin of mixed peas and carrots into a pan and placed it on the hob.

As he waited for the meal to cook, he lit the fire in the lounge because it was starting to get cold. It was the one thing Hamlet had noticed since he'd moved here — how quickly the temperature dropped once the sun went down. And it wasn't as if he could just turn up the thermostat. His heating was down to paper, kindle and logs, which he always made sure he had prepared in the grate, ready for lighting.

He returned to the kitchen, grabbed a beer from the fridge and went to his study.

The study had been specially built for his grandfather by the joiner who'd built the kitchen. It was lined floor to ceiling with oak shelves, crammed with his grandfather's books. Hamlet had spent quite a lot of time in here, watching his grandfather paint, while attempting his own masterpiece with pencils; once the cabin became his, he'd come in here to read when he and Helen had used the cabin as their weekend retreat. It held a lot of memories. Some good and also some bad; happy family photographs were offset by newspaper articles on his family's murders. They littered the huge mahogany desk his grandfather had bought at auction. He'd read them dozens of times over the last three years, mourning and crying over them.

Hamlet had increased his visits to this room recently. It was where he had brought all the research material he'd copied — the newspaper clippings on recent suicides — which is how he'd found the piece in the *Derbyshire Times* about Tanya Hodkin. The piece that had triggered all these events of recent days. Since then, he'd come in here every day making copious notes of his meetings with Alix. The one thing he wanted more than anything was to catch the killer that had murdered his family.

It was almost 10 p.m. before Alix got home. She had driven the entire journey repeatedly checking her rear-view mirror for sign of any vehicle hanging behind her longer than normal. It had even resulted in her going around two of the roundabouts three times and driving into two cul-de-sacs to double-check that no one was following her.

On the way home, she had stopped off at a late-night supermarket to grab an oven-bake lasagne, some salad, fresh bread and milk, and while going around the aisles, she had continually looked over her shoulder, checking out the few customers shopping so late. She had even stopped by the exit, casting her eyes around the car park to see if anyone was lurking, before walking to her car. *I've become one paranoid lady*, she thought to herself, as she placed the carrier bag in the boot.

Alix was usually pretty good at leaving some of the gruesome elements of her work behind when she left the office each night, but right now she felt different; the sight of Frank Mooney's body — one of their own — covered in blood, and the thought that she may have led his killer right to him, was going to stay with her for a long time.

By the time she pulled up outside her home she was drained, and she dragged out her shoulder bag and shopping from the boot as if she was hauling out lead weights. Letting herself into the house, she threw herself back into alert mode. Carefully setting her bags down in the hallway, she locked the door behind her, and with one hand holding tightly onto her police-issue PAVA spray, she went through her usual routine of turning on every light and checking each room, before returning back to the hallway for her shopping, slipping off her shoes, setting the alarm's perimeter zone and going into the kitchen.

She put the lasagne in the oven, set the timer for thirty-five minutes and went to the fridge where she had half a bottle of white wine waiting for her. Grabbing a glass, she poured a large measure and took a good glug, swilling it around her mouth before swallowing. *That's hit the spot.* Then, setting down the glass, she trotted upstairs, turned on the shower and hurriedly undressed out of her work-clothes. Before climbing in, she set the temperature hotter than normal, and after testing that she could bear it, stepped into the cubicle and threw back her head to face the powerful jets.

Within seconds she could feel the stress leaving her body. After a quick soaping and rinse, she climbed out and towelled herself dry. By the time she'd hung up her work suit and put on her lounge top and bottoms, she felt like a different person to the one that had entered her home half an hour ago, and was now looking forward to her late meal.

She entered the kitchen just as the timer on the cooker beeped. *Perfect timing.* She checked the lasagne was cooked, turned off the oven, plated it up with a little salad, and together with her glass of wine, carried it through to the lounge. She set her meal and wine down on the coffee table, picked up the TV remote, selected the feel-good movie she was halfway through, and flopped down onto the sofa, arranging the cushions around her. The lasagne and salad was welcoming, and the chilled wine even more so; so much so that she returned to the fridge and poured herself another large glass, emptying the bottle.

It was after 11.30 p.m. when the movie ended. She put the dirty dishes in the sink, thought about washing them but then decided they could wait until morning. After another quick security check of the downstairs rooms, she turned off the lights and climbed wearily up the stairs to her bedroom. Getting gratefully into bed, Alix was soon asleep.

What was that noise?

That wasn't the sound of the house settling. It sounded like someone was on the landing outside her room; Alix recognised the creaking of the old floorboards underfoot. She bolted upright in the bed, straining her ears in the direction of the sound. There it was again. Someone was definitely making their way slowly across the landing.

She threw her legs out from beneath the duvet and held her breath. Another footfall. Whoever it was outside her door was planting down cautious measured footsteps. She dragged her dressing gown from the bottom of her bed and slipped it on, fastening the belt tightly around her waist. The bed creaked as she rose and the footsteps stopped.

Her heart started hammering against her chest. Moving quickly but with caution, on the balls of her feet, she reached the door of her bedroom, grabbed the handle and turned it slowly. Silence now.

Heart in her throat, Alix threw open the door to be met by a bright light which blinded her.

Alix bolted awake. She was drenched in sweat and her heart was pounding. For a moment she was back at her parents' house, the vicarage in Cambridgeshire, and she was terrified. But then just as quickly, she realised she was actually in her own bedroom and it had just been another nightmare. She took a deep breath of relief. It had been a long time since that dream had visited her. She flashed her eyes around her bedroom, picking out the built-in wardrobes and dressing table in the soothing warm orange glow of the nightlight she kept on whilst she slept: her security blanket to ward off her demons.

As her heartrate started to steady, she wondered what had brought on the nightmare. Had it been the sight of Frank's body? Whatever it was, it had seriously fucked up her head.

She pushed aside her duvet, climbed out of bed and faced herself in the wardrobe mirror. Dressed in her nightdress she could just make out the tramline scars across each of her thighs. The scars of mutilation she had inflicted upon herself in the months and years following her ordeal. Scars that she had put there for a reason; to make sure they would put anyone else off ever doing that to her again.

No one had seen them and she had only ever divulged the secret of what she had done to herself to her counsellor. And yet today, for some strange reason, she had started to open up to Hamlet. If it hadn't been for the phone call from Lauren, she knew she would have told him everything.

EIGHTEEN

In MIT Alix stretched back in her seat and looked around the office. Most of her colleagues were out on enquiries, but the limited few that were in were beavering away at their desks, either on their computers or making phone calls. She had been doing some online research, making phone calls and sending emails since morning briefing, all with a view to exhuming the grave of Elsie Davenport.

A lot had been crammed into morning briefing. Most surprising and interesting of all had been the forensic results from the toxicology screenings of the bloods from Tanya Hodkin and Dr Whitton; both of them showed a test result of ketamine, a potent analgesic. It now appeared that the substance Tanya had snorted, believing it was cocaine, had been nothing of the sort. It was no wonder she had been taken ill.

With regards to Dr Whitton, there would be no way of knowing how the drug had been administered to him, because his body had been cremated. However, it gave them a lead to follow with regards the needle mark found on Frank Mooney's neck. If he had been injected with ketamine then it would explain why he had not put up any kind of fight.

Regarding his murder, the majority of MIT were up at Ringinglow making enquiries, though so far, none had generated any useful leads. They had quickly discovered that the vast majority of the village's residents spent most of the day away at work to pay for their expensive mortgages, and although Frank's neighbours were retired and at home, they hadn't seen or heard anything suspicious. They had also discovered that access to Frank's cottage could be gained quite easily from the rear, as a public footpath ran alongside his low boundary wall. It was a path used frequently by walkers heading to the moors, and faced with that information a decision had been made to put out a televised appeal for witnesses that evening. Lauren Simmerson was up there at the moment with several TV and radio crews.

Next up had been another surprising discovery, this one from the CCTV hard drive they had seized from the bar Tanya had visited the night before her death. Footage had shown her picking something up from the floor by the bar. It wasn't clear precisely what she had picked up, because of the camera distance, but there was no doubt in anyone's mind that it was the ketamine they now knew she had ingested, courtesy of toxicology. What they hadn't got was footage of who had dropped it. There had been a crowd of people around that area at the most likely time it had been dropped; however, one individual stood out as a 'Person of Interest'. A tall, stocky man wearing a padded jacket and jeans, with a mop of dark brown hair and a beard, who kept his head tucked low. He was among the crowd at the bar at the relevant time the package was dropped, and, suspiciously, he didn't buy a drink. Instead, he slipped away with someone who did, quickly separating, and going over alone to an empty table, where he sat with his head bowed.

The footage had been frozen several times during briefing, and while the man certainly fitted the profile of James Harry Benson, in terms of height and build, there was no getting a firm facial identification. What they did see was him getting up from the table and approaching Tanya whilst her friend Sally was at the bar fetching her a glass of water. At this stage, Tanya's head was lolling all over the place and she was struggling to coordinate her legs. The team saw the man place his hands under her arms and calmly shuffle her out of the pub.

It was a key find and the CCTV footage was now on its way to forensics to see if it could be enhanced for facial recognition. So far it was the best lead they had.

With regards to information on Benson that might help to trace him, whilst they had now been emailed a copy of his file from Moor Lodge, there appeared to be nothing in it which would help locate him quickly. Other than a brief mention of his parents being dead, there were no other named family members and no mention of any known associates. It seemed that James Harry Benson was a loner. He was out there, somewhere, with tenuous links to at least seven murders, but with the ability to appear and disappear like a ghost. Something told Alix that this was going to be a very difficult and, more than likely, long-term investigation, but she, more than anyone, was determined to see that the person who had carried out these atrocities was put permanently behind bars. She had made the mistake of believing the killer had been Hamlet, and now she wanted to set that right.

'How's it going?'

DCI Jackson made her jump. She hadn't heard him approach her station. She spun in her chair. 'Crikey boss, don't do that to me.'

He broke into a smile. 'Why? Were you up to no good? Doing some internet shopping?'

'Ha ha, very funny.' She turned back to her screen, 'I'm still trying to sort out the exhumation of Elsie Davenport's grave.' That morning an email had arrived from the funeral directors who had organised Elsie's burial, revealing that her funeral had taken place at Abbey Lane Cemetery — a stone's throw from

Totley Brook Children's Home — on the 23rd December 1995, the same day fourteen-year-old Alice Crompton was last seen. It had immediately reinforced Alix's belief that the recording they had captured through Hamlet's app the previous day was the killer telling them that Alice was dead and buried in Elsie's grave. The moment she had shared this information with Karl Jackson, the DCI had tasked her with arranging an exhumation of Elsie's grave.

'I've just come to see how it's going,' Jackson responded.

'It's a devil of a job you've given me. I thought it would be so simple, a couple of phone calls, a bit of signed paper, and that would be it.'

'And it isn't?' he asked.

'Damn right it isn't. To remove human remains from the ground we have to apply for a licence from the Ministry of Justice, get permission from the Diocesan Court, tell Environmental Health, the cemeteries officer, sort out body removers, oh, and speak with Elsie's family, and that's just for starters.'

'Well that should keep you out of trouble for a few hours.' The DCI released a short chuckle. 'I'm just going for a long relaxing lunch, let me know how you've got on when I get back.'

As he started to walk away, Alix called over her shoulder, 'You can laugh, Boss, but I forgot to tell you, this lot costs a packet. It's going to seriously dent your budget.' She cracked a grin of her own as she lowered her head and returned to filling out the notification form for the Ministry of Justice.

It was still the middle of the night, a good few hours before dawn, and Hamlet was standing in Abbey Lane Cemetery surrounded by cops, forensic officers, and officials from the local council, overlooking two police officers in boiler suits digging up a grave. Arc lights on tripods gave everything a top-lit, silhouette effect, enhancing the ground mist that was swirling around the cemetery. The only sound in the graveyard was a mushy thump and sucking noise as shovels delved into clods of damp earth. It was surreal. Hamlet felt like a bit actor in a Hammer Horror movie.

He hadn't asked to be here. Alix had requested that he attend. She had rung him that evening on her way home from work to tell him what was happening and asked him to meet her at the cemetery. After introducing Hamlet to her DCI, she handed him a forensic suit and he was now dressed in a white all-in-one, huddled around Elsie Davenport's grave, buzzing with anticipation. He had only ever seen an exhumation on television.

The officers had carefully removed each shovelful of soil and piled it to one side for the forensic team to scrutinise, only scooping out another when they were given the nod. They had been going for over an hour and were now in a hole up to their knees. Hamlet had been surprised at how slow and methodical the procedure was. Nothing at all like on television. He was starting to feel the cold, his feet especially, but didn't dare stamp them to warm up because he didn't want to bring attention to himself. He felt privileged that he had been invited, as though he was part of Alix's investigation team, and didn't want to do anything that would announce his presence. He had already seen the reaction in the other officers' faces when Alix had introduced him.

Hamlet's eyes were fixed firmly on the diggers. They worked slowly because of the dampness of the earth, their brows bathed in a sweaty sheen.

Suddenly a call went up from the taller of the two gravediggers. 'Got something,' he said excitedly, placing his shovel on the ground above the trench. He began to climb out, followed by his shorter colleague, and two of the observing forensic team took their place.

One of them dropped onto his haunches, and Hamlet could make out from his arm movement that he was wiping away loose bits of topsoil. After a few seconds he stopped, gave a quick nod to his colleague, and then gazed over to where Alix and Hamlet were standing.

'It looks like we've got something,' he said.

Hamlet went to take a step forward but Alix pulled him back swiftly, a firm hand on his arm.

'Forensics will take it from here, Hamlet. We wait,' she whispered into his ear.

He nodded and shuffled back into position.

From then on, events sped up. CSI officers, who had so far been bystanders, swung into action. Within minutes they had erected a large blue tent over the excavated grave. Then the arc lights were removed and re-positioned inside the tent. Except for Hamlet and Alix, everyone slipped inside, and thanks to the intense bright lighting inside the tent, Hamlet watched a series of obscure shadows play out a show reminiscent of an old-fashioned silhouette performance loved by the Victorians. Nobody seemed to stand still for a moment. The only time anyone appeared was when one of them brought out a barrow load of soil, piled it close to the entrance and then disappeared back inside again.

The team were still toiling away as dawn appeared above the rooftops of the houses backing onto the cemetery. Watching the orange glow split open the grey sky was a very calming experience for Hamlet. He found himself becoming emotionally overwhelmed by the situation, so much so, that he dipped his head so no one saw the tears welling up. Discreetly wiping them away with an arm, he suddenly became aware of a sound behind him. It was the sound of feet scuffing dried leaves and he turned. There were several bright flashes, causing Hamlet to shield is eyes. As his vision cleared, he could make out two human shapes a few yards away.

'Is Dr Mottrell a suspect again, Detectives? Is he showing you where he's buried more bodies?'

Hamlet recognised the voice before his eyes revealed who was doing the talking. Kieran Croft.

'How the fuck did he get in here?' snarled DCI Jackson.

Alix set off at a sprint towards the journalist and cameraman.

There was another camera flash and Hamlet spun away. *Bastards!* Then, half-turning, he was just in time to see Alix push the crime correspondent against a tall headstone.

She jabbed a finger in Kieran's face. 'What the fuck are you doing here?' she growled.

The journalist's face wore a wicked smirk.

'The public have a right to know if Dr Mottrell is involved in more deaths, Detective.'

Alix dropped her finger, but kept Kieran Croft braced awkwardly against the gravestone. 'This is a police investigation, Mr Croft, and you are obstructing our enquiries. I will give you and your cameraman exactly thirty seconds to make yourselves scarce or I will arrest you. Do I make myself clear?'

'As a bell, Detective,' Kieran responded, holding up his hands in surrender. He squirmed away from her, sauntering cockily back to the path that led to the entrance gates. The cameraman followed.

'You come anywhere near my crime scene again, Mr Croft, and your feet won't touch the fucking ground,' Alix shouted after him.

'Is that a quote, Detective?' called back the journalist.

After the encounter with Kieran, DCI Jackson called in more troops to beef up security around the cemetery whilst the forensics team continued to go about their job. The cadaver they unearthed in Elsie Davenport's grave definitely wasn't Elsie. First, the body lay only a few feet beneath the ground, second it wasn't in a coffin, and third, everything about it, from the dark hair still attached to the decaying head, to the jeans and top the corpse was clothed in, told them it was almost certainly that of missing fourteen-year-old Alice Crompton.

Watching the exhumation had been a fascinating experience for Hamlet, in spite of the press interruption. He had no real knowledge of what to expect, but the emotional feeling it brought about was not what he had anticipated at all; watching the forensic team painstakingly excavate the corpse, placing it inside a body bag, and then loading it into the waiting private ambulance with such dignity, brought about another tear. Hamlet knew this was going to rake up more misery for a family.

After watching the ambulance steadily drive away, Alix had turned to Hamlet and told him she had a lot to do, which he took as a signal that he was no longer needed. Handing back his forensic suit, he drove home, deep in thought. A lot of his thoughts were taken up by the ambush by Kieran Croft. How he'd managed to find out about the exhumation and its location was now worrying him. Had someone on the investigation team tipped him off, just to make his life an even bigger misery? He could only think that there might still be detectives who were still questioning his guilt. Hamlet discounted Alix. He firmly believed that she was now on his side because of what they had gone through together in recent days.

It was coming up to 9 a.m. by the time Hamlet got home, and he was wired. Lucky greeted him eagerly and after making a quick fuss of the little dog, Hamlet took him for his morning walk. The stroll had the desired effect; by the time they got back to the cabin Hamlet could feel himself becoming weary, and after putting out some food and fresh water for the dog he made himself a bacon sandwich and then sank onto the sofa, allowing Lucky to snuggle up beside him. After listening to his gentle snores for ten minutes, Hamlet closed his eyes.

NINETEEN

It was 2 p.m. when Hamlet's phone woke him with a start. It was Alix. She told him she was coming straight from work to update him and he was instantly buoyed. He grabbed a quick shower and tidied around the place, before heading down to the gate with Lucky. Alix arrived shortly after 5 p.m. and as he keyed open the padlock he flashed her a smile. The smile she returned was weak, instantly filling him with unease. He let her drive through and after securing the gate, he picked up Lucky and climbed into the passenger seat.

Hamlet met her gaze. 'Something up?'

'I'll show you when we get to the cabin.'

After pulling into the clearing, they sat for a moment with the engine idling.

'I'm guessing you haven't seen the evening paper?' Alix said.

A recollection of that morning's ambush by Kieran Croft in the cemetery swept through Hamlet's mind and a feeling of dread crept over him. 'What's he done now?'

She reached across and picked up a newspaper from the back seat, slapping it into his hand. 'Take a deep breath before you explode.'

Hamlet was greeted by the front-page headline, 'SHEFFIELD EXHUMATION 24 YEARS AFTER GIRL WENT MISSING' and below that was a picture of himself graveside next to a shocked-looking Alix and her DCI, the three of them garbed like Michelin Men. Below that was the strapline, '*Doctor Death assisting detectives with their enquiries.*' He let out an irritated sigh. That, technically, wasn't a lie, but the implication was entirely opposite to the truth. He read on:

Officials are unsure whether a grave exhumed today in a Sheffield cemetery contains the body of missing schoolgirl, 14-year-old Alice Crompton, who went missing in December 1995. Coroner, Brian Seagrave, said that until the pathologist and the police have carried out their investigation, he is unable to comment.

Hamlet could read no further. He felt sick. He threw the paper back onto the rear seat in disgust.

'I guessed you'd react like that,' said Alix.

'I ought to sue him for writing stuff like this. It's defamatory.'

'We've no idea how he's managed to find out about Alice Crompton. Just before I came here the DCI had us all in for briefing to see how Kieran had got hold of this information, and I'd like to assure you that I'm confident when I say nothing has been leaked by anyone from MIT. We think the story about Alice has come from one of the residents, or the former children's home staff we've spoken to. And with regards to the exhumation, we had to notify the Coroner's Office and the Local Authority, and they get regular press enquiries, so we think that's how he found out about that.

'The good thing is that Kieran hasn't linked it to Frank's death, or Thomas Midgley's,' Alix continued, adding, 'though no doubt he's trying to join the dots, and will do so the minute we officially release James Harry Benson's name as a person of interest.'

Hamlet let out a deep breath, 'And that's when it starts all over again — the regurgitation of my involvement in Benson's release from Moor Lodge and the murders of my family.'

'I'm sorry, Hamlet.'

He let out another long sigh. 'It's not your fault. I just wish he would leave me alone. Why is he doing this? I've been through enough pain already.'

'If it's any comfort, I've spoken with the DCI and he's agreed that once we receive confirmation that the body in the grave is Alice, then we're putting out a press statement exonerating you from our enquiries. We are going to go big on seeking publicity on Benson's whereabouts. That should get Kieran off your back.'

'I really hope so, Alix. I don't know how much more of this I can put up with. I could easily wring Kieran's neck.'

'Well, don't do it whilst I'm on duty.'

That made him laugh, instantly lifting his spirits. 'Do you have to rush off?' he asked.

She gave him a curious glance. 'Why?'

'I was going to offer you a drink, seeing as you've taken the time to drive out here to tell me this.'

'Well, I don't have any pressing engagements, if that's what you're asking. And I'm officially off duty, so I gladly accept your offer.'

'This is cosy,' said Alix, taking a sip of her wine.

Hamlet watched her holding the glass by the stem and swirling the contents around, eyeing it like a connoisseur. The flames licking the back of the grate made a wonderful backdrop, and he hadn't turned on the light so they were bathed in a warm orange glow.

'It's a mix of two grapes. French. One of my favourites,' he told her.

'Are you trying to impress me with your wine selection, Hamlet?'

He released a hearty laugh. He kept a number of decent wines stored in the cool larder at the back of the kitchen but hadn't touched any of them since Helen's death. In fact, he hadn't shared wine with anyone for the past three years and he was so glad Alix had accepted his invite.

Alix took another sip. 'This must have been a lovely weekend retreat…' She pulled herself up. 'Sorry, that was a bit insensitive. I didn't think.'

Hamlet held up his hand. 'Don't worry. I know how you meant it to sound. And yes, it was a lovely retreat for us. The best times were always in autumn and winter. We'd sit just like this. Outside, it could be as foul as it wanted to be, and Helen and I would sit in front of the fire, warm as toast, getting drunk on nice wine.' He smiled at the memories.

'How did you meet Helen, if you don't mind me asking?'

His gaze drifted to the fire, watching the dancing flames. One of the logs tumbled slightly, sending up a shower of sparks. 'We met when I was doing locum work. I got a job in A&E at the Northern General and Helen was a staff nurse there.'

'Doctors and nurses, eh!'

'I suppose you could say that. It was love at first sight for me — if that doesn't sound too corny?'

'No, corny's good.' She took another drink. 'And how long before you were married?'

'Just over eighteen months. You could say it was a whirlwind romance. We rented a flat together at first, whilst I was studying to be a psychologist, and then once I qualified, thanks to the inheritance from my grandfather, I bought the house in Arbourthorne. It needed some work on it, but Helen took it on as a project, and threw herself into it while I was working all hours God sent, and, well, she made it our home. You saw how it was, didn't you?'

Alix nodded. 'Yes, it was beautiful. I've got an old Victorian semi — not as big as the one you had — but it's a nice comfortable house, and I'm gradually making it into a home, but like your job, I'm working more hours than I wish.'

'Do you live with anyone?'

Alix shook her head, swiftly raising her glass to her mouth and finishing her wine in one mouthful.

Hamlet thought he detected a look of concern and he was instantly reminded of their previous conversation, and although he didn't want to push her because of the sensitivity of the subject, he was curious to know what had happened. Before he decided to say anything, he topped up her glass and refreshed his own.

Taking a sip, Hamlet noticed Alix was avoiding looking at him and the silence between them was growing. He decided to break it, 'I hope I haven't touched a nerve, Alix. I've just remembered our last conversation. I'm sorry if I have.'

Alix took a heavy breath. 'It's okay, Hamlet, and you are entitled to ask me, seeing as it was me who raised it in the first place, though God knows why I did. You must have caught me at a vulnerable moment. You're the only person I've told about what happened to me, besides the police in Cambridge and my counsellor.' She took another breath, held it for a moment and released it slowly. 'It was ten years ago and I haven't had a relationship since then. But I have been close with someone recently. Very close. With a colleague. But that ended badly. Story of my life.' Her gaze was fixed on the blazing log fire.

Hamlet caught the sadness in her voice and saw that her eyes had glassed over. He left it a few seconds then said, 'Do you want to talk about it? I'm a good listener, and I promise that what's said here, stays here, if that's any reassurance.'

Alix held the rim of her glass against her lips, deep in thought. 'It does help to talk about it, Hamlet. It hurts when I do, but at the same time it helps. I always feel sick when I talk about it.'

'If you don't want to say anything, you don't have to. We can just sit here and enjoy the fire and the wine. I'll never say another word about it.'

Alix took another drink. 'The colleague I was involved with was Sam. Sam Reese. He was my tutor when I was a probationer and then we teamed up together on a regular basis.' She paused and gave a half laugh. 'Works love affair, just like yours.'

Hamlet returned a smile.

'And this is where it gets to confession time. He was married.'

'Dangerous ground there,' Hamlet responded.

'I know. I should have run a mile, but it wasn't as straight forward as that. Things weren't going well between him and his wife. She was in the job as well. A detective at Rotherham. He suspected she was having an affair. Someone had tipped him off about it and he'd apparently found a few suspicious texts on her phone. There were rows, and he used to tell me about them when we were in the car and sometimes after work in the pub. I was just a sounding board at first but I couldn't help but feel sorry for him.' She paused, studied Hamlet's face for a moment and said, 'I know what you're thinking! Sob story to get me into bed.'

Hamlet shook his head. 'I'm not thinking anything, Alix. I'm just listening. There's no judgement.'

'If you want to know, it was me who fell for him.' She took another sip of wine. 'Though nothing happened between us. Before it got to that stage, he was killed.'

Hamlet was shocked. 'Oh, I'm so sorry to hear that, Alix. Was it an accident at work?'

She shook her head slowly. 'At work, yes. But it wasn't an accident. He was stabbed.'

'That's terrible!'

'What made it worse was I was there. Guess you could say wrong time, wrong place.'

'You don't have to continue with this, if it holds such bad memories.'

'No, I need to, now I've started. Like I say it exorcises my demons. But I'll need another drink.' She held up her empty glass and issued a tight smile.

Hamlet looked towards the bottle. It was empty. He pushed himself up off the sofa. 'We've seen it off. I'll need to open another bottle,' he said and gave her a questioning look. 'I'm thinking about you driving home.'

'We'll think about that when we come to it. Besides, with a fire like this and your comfortable sofa, I can always crash here, can't I?'

Hamlet shot her a surprised look. 'You're more than welcome to crash here. I've got a spare room with a bed. It'll need a bit of airing, but I've got a hot water bottle that'll take care of that.'

'That's sorted then,' she responded, holding up her empty glass. 'More wine it is.'

Hamlet uncorked another bottle of red and brought it through. 'It's a long time since I've drunk as much as this,' he said. 'I bet I have a thick head tomorrow.'

'As long as you have no regrets.'

He thought about that for just a second and then shook his head. 'Do you know, I think I might have deserved this night? The last three years have been a nightmare I haven't been able to wake up from. Although I think *you* believe me now, I can tell from some of your colleagues faces that *they* don't.'

Alix eyed him a moment. 'To be blunt, Hamlet, until we actually prove you weren't responsible for what happened to your family, you will always be under suspicion.'

'Does that mean you don't believe me?'

'Would I be here, drinking wine with you, if I thought you were a murderer?'

Alix cocked her head, reminding Hamlet of Lucky whenever he eyed him with inquisitiveness. He decided not to pursue this conversation. He was more interested in what she had to tell him and so replenished both their glasses from the new bottle and then set it down on the hearth. Crackling came from the grate as flames licked the new log that Alix had added. The fire was belting out some heat, and he felt more relaxed than he had in a long time. He raised his glass to Alix, took a glug and said, 'You were saying about Sam?'

'Yes, Sam. I'd fallen in love with him, and he didn't even get to know it, because some bastard killed him.' She looked far away for a few seconds, then she continued. 'We were on afters, about to drive back to the nick to go off duty, but I needed some milk and Sam wanted some beers so we called in at a convenience store we regularly used. Sam got out of the car first and I was just getting my purse out of my bag when I heard Sam shout. I looked up just as this guy in a hoodie and scarf ran past the car. I saw Sam on his knees and by the time I got out of the car the guy was disappearing round the corner. When I turned back, Sam was lying on the ground and blood was everywhere. He'd been stabbed. In the neck. I tried to help, but I couldn't stem the blood. By the time the ambulance reached us, Sam was dead. He died in my arms.'

'Oh no, Alix!'

'We think the guy had been about to rob the store and we'd disturbed him. I just wish I'd have been out of the car as well. Things might just have been different. The guilt has been awful. I didn't just lose a colleague, but someone I cared for, and I never got to tell him.'

Alix and Hamlet stared at one another in silence, mentally sharing each other's grief and pain. Hamlet was the first to haul his gaze away, turning to the fire, watching the flickering flames turn into smoke and disappear up the chimney. He finished his wine in two mouthfuls and poured another glass. He returned his gaze to Alix and saw that her glass was now empty as well and poured her a generous measure.

'Well that's one reason to get drunk, if nothing else,' she said. 'It dulls the pain for a few hours.' Swallowing a good mouthful, she added, 'We're a right pair of morbid buggers, aren't we?'

'President of the Glee Club, me.'

Alix almost spat out her mouthful of wine. She wiped a dribble from the corner of her mouth. 'Sorry about that, Hamlet, I think I'm starting to get drunk.'

'You and me both.' He paused and looked at her. Her face had a lovely pink glow, and under different circumstances he could see himself being attracted to her, though this was definitely not the right time and he quickly dismissed the thought from his mind. He said, 'That story is truly awful Alix.'

'I haven't told you about my attack yet, which is what started this conversation.'

'You don't have to. Another time maybe?'

'No, I'm on a roll now.' She released a nervous giggle. 'I need to get it off my chest and then get hammered. And, I'll hold you to your word.'

'My word?'

'What's said here, stays here.'

He held up two fingers side-by-side, 'Scouts honour.'

Alix turned away from Hamlet, switching her gaze to the fire. 'It happened when I was nineteen.' Her voice was soft, the words considered. 'I was at Sheffield University studying social work and we had broken up for the summer.' Pausing, she continued, 'Just after getting my place at Sheffield, Dad was given a new parish. A village, a few miles from Cambridge, and so Mum and Dad moved down there and I went into rooms near the uni. After they moved it was a few months before I got to see them, because they were settling in, and I was enjoying my own freedom.

'The first time I visited them, I couldn't believe how gorgeous the vicarage was — well, it was to die for. Think the Vicar of Dibley's cottage, and you've got the idea. But I only visited a couple of times, because of the long drive, so the first time I actually got to stay with them was during my summer break. For two months it was just the most idyllic place. It was somewhere you could only ever dream of living. I had a wonderful time, meeting new people and totally chilling. Mum and Dad are into pub quizzes in a big way, and they'd found one in the next village and so I started going with them.

'One night, we came back from the quiz, and I was busting for the loo, so when we got in I ran up to the bathroom. When I was coming back down I heard Mum scream and ran into the lounge to see what was the matter. There was a man wearing a ski mask and he had a knife. We learned later from the police that he had broken in through the study window.'

'That must have been terrifying.'

She gave Hamlet a quick glance, nodded, and returned to looking at the fire. 'It was. He started shouting and threatening us, waving the knife around. I was terrified. Then he started asking Dad where all the money was. But we didn't have any. One of the church wardens dealt with all the cash from services and Dad's pay was a pittance. Dad told him that we hadn't got anything worth stealing, but he didn't believe him and started smacking him across the face.

'I screamed for him to stop and he turned on me. He stuck his knife under my chin and starting threatening to cut me if I didn't do as I was told. I have never been so terrified in all my life. That's when Mum said she had some jewellery upstairs in her bedroom. He tied Mum and Dad up and then told me to show him where it was. In that moment I knew what was going to happen. Before he forced me upstairs, I remember looking at my dad, pleading with him to help me, but he didn't move. He just sat there. And then the man pushed me upstairs and raped me. And what was worse, afterwards, he said to me, "I'm sorry. It wasn't meant to be like this".'

Alix lowered her glass and turned slowly to face Hamlet. It seemed as if she was staring straight through him and he felt a shiver down his back. 'Oh, Alix, that is the most awful experience. I can't imagine what you went through.' His words of empathy seemed to drag her back from wherever she had been and he could see that he once again had her full attention. 'Did they catch him?'

Her mouth tightened. 'No, not as far as I'm aware. If they have, he's not confessed to the police what he did to me. From time to time I search the internet to see if there are any similar cases. I've come across a couple of cases that are similar, but he got away. As far as I'm aware, he's still out there, but I'm determined that one day I will face him.'

'I'd like to be a fly on the wall when that happens.' Hamlet gave a half-laugh in an attempt to put some light-heartedness back into the conversation. It seemed to have worked, for she released her own small laugh and he studied her face as their eyes engaged. He held her gaze for a few seconds and then said, 'Can I share something with you, now you've told me all that?'

She gave him a curious look. 'Y-e-s,' she answered slowly.

'Before you told me what happened, I actually thought you were going to tell me that it was your dad who raped you.'

'My Dad! Whatever made you think that?'

'The way you speak about him. There's anger there.'

'Yes, there's anger. As I said, when the man told me to go upstairs, I expected my dad to do something, to come to my aid, but he didn't. And since it happened things have not been the same between us. I can't look him in the eye and, to be honest, I've lost my faith in him.' She paused and said, 'I know that sounds awful and I know he's a man of God and all that, but he's still my dad, and dads should protect their children, shouldn't they?'

Hamlet nodded, understanding her feelings. 'Maybe you should talk to him about the way you feel. He's probably hurting inside himself.'

Her mouth tightened and she looked as though she was about to burst into tears. Shrugging her shoulders, she said, 'Maybe. I need to go and see him. I've promised Mum I will,' and she downed her wine.

TWENTY

Alix bolted awake. Something had disturbed her and the intense darkness caused confusion, throwing her into a sudden panic. Then she remembered where she was; Hamlet's spare bedroom.

As she rolled over, wondering why she had woken with such a start, her head started to thump and the inside of her mouth felt as if it was loaded with cotton wool. The events of the previous night filled her head and she cursed herself for polishing off the second bottle of wine. She had never been able to take her drink. She was going to feel rough in the morning if she didn't do something about it. She reached for the glass of water on the bedside table and drank it down in one go.

She had shared things with Hamlet that she'd only ever shared with her counsellor and with the detectives who had investigated her rape, and now she felt remorse and a sense of embarrassment. Should she get up and sneak away? It felt like a good idea. It would give her some breathing space and distance. Though, even if she did slip away now, she would still have to face him again at some stage. Why on earth had she told him? It had to be the wine that had made her open up.

She shook her head. It wasn't just the alcohol, or the way his sparkling blue eyes had dazzled her. No, it was down to the fact that she trusted Hamlet with her secret. And, more than that, she felt comfortable with him knowing. More than with Sam. And that was unsettling. Hamlet was still technically a suspect in a multiple murder investigation, although she no longer believed that he was responsible for the deaths. Nevertheless, she shouldn't be having these feelings.

Get a grip girl. What are you thinking?

The scars on the inside of her thighs started to nag. She reached down to touch them — to stroke the marks of self-mutilation that she'd inflicted on herself in the vain hope that it would put off any other would-be rapist from doing the same to her again. The moment she touched the first ugly welt, visions of that night ten years ago crashed into her brain. The dark eyes of her attacker, staring coldly through the gaps in his ski mask, oblivious to the pain he was causing her. She still suffered anxiety attacks, and regularly woke up in the middle of the night lathered in sweat, her demon never far from the surface, though they had occurred a lot less of late. Until now.

She took a deep breath and let it out slowly. She repeated the exercise numerous times until her heart rate settled back into its normal rhythm. The thump in her head returned. She needed another glass of water. As she swung her legs out of bed, she dismissed thoughts of slipping away. Facing Hamlet in the morning would be her first test to see if she could cope. Besides, there was something about Hamlet that made her feel good about herself again.

Hamlet had heard Alix get up in the middle of the night. He'd also heard Lucky traipsing after her, the sounds of his claws clipping the wooden floor. She hadn't shooed him away and he'd smiled. The little dog had a new friend.

He had been lying awake for a good hour before he heard Alix's bedroom door open. Listening to the shower hiss against the cubicle, Hamlet slipped out of bed, threw on a T-shirt, pulled on his joggers, and made his way to the kitchen, where he filled up the kettle and switched it on. He spooned coffee into two mugs, took some bread out of the freezer and popped two slices into the toaster. His head felt woolly and he took two paracetamols, downing them with water, hoping that would do the trick. He didn't want to be nursing a thick head for the rest of the day.

As the kettle boiled, Alix emerged from the bathroom scrunching her hair in a towel. She was dressed in the grey suit trousers and white tailored shirt she had worn yesterday and he was surprised to see hardly a crease in them. She looked remarkably fresh given her night of drink.

'You wouldn't have a brush by any chance?' she asked, squeezing her brown hair in the towel.

He did have one. It had belonged to Helen. He nodded, hurried back to his bedroom, found it straight away and brought it back for Alix. Then he watched her out of the corner of his eye, brushing out the knots of her damp hair. It brought back memories of Helen doing the same thing. He quickly pushed the thought aside, picking up one of the steaming mugs and placing it in front of her. She thanked him with a smile and pulled her hair up into a ponytail.

Hamlet took out the toast, buttered it, then put two more pieces of bread into the toaster.

'Thank you, Hamlet. This is much appreciated.' She secured her ponytail with a scrunchy and flicked it over the collar of her shirt. 'That spare bed of yours is very comfortable. I was out like a light.'

'I think that might have been the wine and not the bed.' He laughed.

'You're probably right,' she chuckled back and took a drink of her coffee. 'Anyway, what are you doing with your day?' she asked, setting down her mug and picking up one of the rounds of toast.

'I'm taking Lucky for his walk and then I'm going to sit down and wrack my brains to see if I can think of anything that might lead to the whereabouts of James Harry Benson. I know a little about his family, and about his time at the children's home, from the sessions I had with him, though it wasn't in any great detail because he was so evasive, but I'm hoping it will trigger something to help you.' He took a drink of coffee, holding the mug in both hands, finding the warmth gratifying. The cabin was always cold first thing in the morning, and even though he had lived here for three years, he still hadn't got used to it. 'What are your plans for the day?'

'Probably manic as ever,' she replied, raising her eyebrows. 'We've still got a fair bit of work with Frank's murder — we still have well over half the village to speak to, and that's before we even start with Alice Crompton. I wouldn't be surprised if we have to call in some help on this one, given how many deaths there are to investigate. I've never known anything like it.' She bit off a chunk of her toast. 'And thank you again for this,' she muttered, her mouth half full. 'And for last night.' Alix's eyes locked on to Hamlet's. 'I found it so easy to talk to you. It was really helpful.'

'I'm glad. I'm happy to help.'

She finished her toast, took another long drink and set down her mug without finishing her coffee. 'I'm afraid I've got to go, Hamlet. Briefing's at eight and I can't be late for that.' She slipped past him, touching his shoulder. 'I'll just get my things together.'

Hamlet watched her make her way towards the spare bedroom, Lucky trotting after her, so close to her heels he was afraid the little dog might trip her up. She emerged with her jacket on and her bag over her shoulder.

'I'll put my face on when I get in to work,' she said, making for the door.

He slipped the padlock key from its hook in the lounge, hurriedly pulled on his trainers and made his way across the lounge. 'I'll need to let you out,' he said, as she opened the door.

'Crikey, I forgot about the gate.'

As Alix popped the lock on her car and climbed in, Hamlet picked up Lucky and got into the front passenger seat. Reversing a few yards, she locked the steering into a half turn and drove onto the track that took them down to the gate. A couple of minutes later, they pulled up in front of the gate and Hamlet got out, unlocked the padlock and yanked open the gate. As she drove slowly through, she wound down her window, offering him a warm smile. 'I'll be in touch to let you know how things are going,' she said, giving a quick wave.

Hamlet wanted to ask, *When are you dropping by again?* Instead, he held up his hand in a farewell gesture and said, 'Be in touch, Alix, and good luck with everything. Hope you catch him soon.'

'Me too,' she replied, heading towards the road.

Hamlet needed to blow away the cobwebs after the night's indulgence and headed into the woods, where, though cold, the sun was starting to break through, and that suited him this morning — the walk would freshen him. He took the track up to the Neolithic burial chamber at the uppermost part of his wood, setting a good pace.

Lucky explored almost every bush and sniffed at every tree, while Hamlet took in the smells of the woodland, particularly the strong smell of pine, allowing his thoughts to drift.

Alix's visit had stirred up a lot of memories, some happy and some sad, and snapshots of them drifted in and out of his mind during the trek. The interviews he'd conducted at the secure unit with James Harry Benson had been part of his recollections, but he's found it hard to drill down on any particular aspect because of the other distractions swirling around in his thoughts.

By the time Hamlet had come to the end of the walk the headache, caused by his hangover, had increased, and he knew he needed some fluids inside him and two more paracetamols quickly if he was to curb the thudding that had started up inside his head. Upping his pace, he took a shortcut back to the cabin, but as he entered the clearing, something didn't feel right.

It was Lucky who initially grabbed his attention. The little dog pulled up sharp, ten yards from the cabin, his sight set on the front door, a ridge of hair rising along his back — a warning sign that diverted Hamlet's gaze to the veranda and then the front door. It was ajar. And he certainly remembered closing it behind him when they had left the cabin.

Someone's in my home.

Dropping his pace, wary of what might be waiting for him, he took each step tentatively as he edged closer. Lucky gave a low growl and tucked in beside him. Spotting his wood axe, he grabbed it up, quickly tested its weight and sturdiness and then moved on. A few yards from the veranda he noticed mud on the steps leading to the door, and, dropping to a snail's pace, slowly mounted them, avoiding the creaky second step. Stopping on the porch, he listened. There wasn't a sound, but he noted that the ridge on Lucky's back was still raised.

His heart banging against his chest, Hamlet gave the door a push with his foot, gripping the axe tighter, ready to take a swing. Inside were more muddy prints, and he saw that his sofa had been pushed aside and the coffee table tossed against the far wall. The room, though, was empty, and he saw that the prints branched off to the right where his study was, the door to it slightly ajar.

Lucky growled and then barked, his entire body rigid. It made Hamlet jump. Suddenly, the dog bolted for the study and Hamlet yelled after him. For a second he debated going after him, but it was only a brief hesitation. He had to protect him and, raising the axe, he darted after Lucky, calling his name as he kicked open the study door.

There were sheets of paper everywhere. The notes Hamlet had made about Tanya Hodkin, together with photographs of Helen and his parents that normally sat on his desk, were scattered across the floor. Lucky was barking frantically at the corner by the large bookshelf, an area deep in shadow because the curtains had been drawn. Something was there but Hamlet couldn't make out what.

The hair on his neck stood up and his heart was hammering ten to the dozen. Ready to strike with the axe, he reached for the light switch and flicked it on.

Kieran Croft was sat in his captain's chair, his head slumped on his chest. It took Hamlet a moment to register that Kieran wasn't moving, and then he realised why. The journalist's hands were cable-tied to the arms of the chair and blood was everywhere. Most of it covered his forearms and hands, but quite a lot was dripping to the floor, forming a pool around him.

His wrists had been slashed.

Hamlet's heart leapt into his mouth.

There was a noise; the rear door slamming.

The killer is still here.

Hamlet spun around, straining his ears. Taking another quick look at the crime correspondent's dead body, Hamlet dashed back the way he had come, sprinting through the lounge and flinging one of the French doors open so hard that the handle slipped from his grasp, clattering against the wall. Behind him, he thought he could hear footsteps, and he leapt from the top step of the veranda down to the ground, landing heavily on mulched leaves that slipped beneath him, causing him to lose his footing and dropping him onto his backside with a thud, a sharp pain shooting up his spine.

Without looking back, he launched himself up, wincing at the pain, and bolted in the direction of the stream, Lucky scampering beside him. At the stream, he dashed across a part that he knew was only ankle deep and then dragged himself up the banking on the other side, cursing as he lost the axe in the water as he scrambled up.

As he clawed to the top he glanced back quickly but couldn't see anyone. At the top of the bank, he set off again at a run. His lungs were starting to burn.

With Lucky beside him he turned in the direction of the Neolithic burial chamber, where the rocky outcrop would give him cover and some much needed breathing space. As the rocks came into view, he quickly sought out which of the boulders would be best to hide behind and threw himself behind it, hitting the ground with a thump and jarring his back again.

Ignoring the pain, he grabbed Lucky and hugged him close to prevent him from barking, and then, trying to steady his breathing, he trained his ears back the way they had come.

Listening.

TWENTY-ONE

Ten minutes later, Hamlet scoured the trees but saw nothing untoward. With no sign of imminent danger, he slowly pushed himself up, testing his back and legs as he straightened. His coccyx, which had taken the brunt of two bad landings, hurt like hell. He also saw that his hands were bleeding from having clawed his way up the banking by the stream.

He let Lucky down and whispered, 'Okay, boy?'

The little dog cocked his head to one side, giving Hamlet his usual placid expression.

What the fuck has just happened? How has Kieran Croft's dead body ended up in my study? Who is the killer I disturbed? Kieran's murder bore the hallmarks of Thomas Midgley and Frank Mooney and one name dominated his thoughts. James Harry Benson.

He needed to phone the police and he needed to get hold of Alix. He pulled his mobile from his pocket and dialled 999. The operator answered within seconds and he blurted out what had happened without drawing breath. She asked him to slow down and explain again, which he did, this time breathing between sentences. She told him to 'hang on, not to touch anything,' and that, 'someone would be with him soon.' Before she hung up, he told her how awkward it was to find his place and said that he would meet them by his gate.

Hamlet stared at his phone. He was starting to shake and his mind was racing, his thoughts tripping over one another. In the time it had taken him to walk around the woods this morning with Lucky, his nemesis, journalist Kieran Croft, had somehow appeared on his property, been tied to a chair in his study, and had his wrists slashed.

Hamlet shook his head in disbelief.

He was about to make his way down to the gate when he remembered the other murder scenes. *I wonder if a message has been left?* He thought of the instructions the operator had just given him not to touch anything, but curiosity was also gnawing away at him.

Recovering his axe from the stream, he cautiously made his way back to the cabin, stopping every fifty yards to listen. As he stepped into the clearing, he came to a halt. For a moment he stood there, running his eyes over the front veranda. The French doors were wide open and his breathing became rapid as the nerves returned. It crossed Hamlet's mind that the killer could still be in there, but common sense told him that he would be very foolish if he was. The killer must surely realise that the police were on their way, and on that thought he edged forwards, climbing the steps to the veranda.

He saw the muddy footprints and, stepping over them, he entered the cabin, raising his axe. Sweeping his eyes around the room they came to a halt when he saw what he had been looking for. Above the fireplace, smudged across the coarse stone in what looked like blood, were the words #YouCan'tHide, and beneath that the sentence 'Seek, and ye shall find.'

Hands shaking, Hamlet activated the app on his mobile, and as soon as the circle of balls started pulsating, he began to scan the graffiti. Nothing. He tried again. Still nothing.

He turned and looked around the room. Except for the upturned coffee table and shifted sofa, everything looked normal. Although he wasn't enthusiastic about seeing Kieran Croft's dead body again, he knew he should check if there was anything in the study which would give an indication as to what happened to the journalist.

He returned to his study, placing his feet carefully to avoid the muddy footprints on the floor as he went. Inside the room, his gaze instantly went to the scattered paperwork and photographs on the floor around his desk — there had obviously been some sort of tussle or fight between the killer and Kieran Croft and the journalist had lost.

That thought instantly cued his gaze upon Kieran tied to the chair. More blood had pooled around him in the forty minutes he had been away and it was beginning to look like brown sludge. Recalling the banging rear door, he could only assume that he had disturbed the killer before he had had time to leave his message.

'My job's done here,' he muttered to himself. 'The police need to do theirs.' He hoped that Alix would be one of the detectives who turned up.

'Come on Lucky,' he called and headed out of the cabin, picking up his car keys as he left. He drove down to the gate, where he parked up, unlocked the padlock and waited.

Hamlet wasn't there long; less than five minutes. A patrol car, blue lights flashing, and an unmarked car, headlights blazing, appeared within seconds of one another, skidding to a halt in front of the gate. He was disappointed to see that Alix wasn't in any of the vehicles, and doubly so when he spotted the driver of the unmarked car was the fresh-faced Nate Fox, who hadn't been too friendly towards him on the previous occasions they had met.

The detective jumped out of the car. 'You made a 999 call about someone being dead?' he said quick-fire.

Hamlet nodded and thumbed back up the track. 'It's the reporter, Kieran Croft. I found him three-quarters of an hour ago in my cabin. It's like the others, he's had his wrists slashed.'

'You told the dispatcher you disturbed someone?'

Hamlet felt his heart rate picking up again. 'I think so, but I'm not exactly sure. I heard the rear door bang when I found Kieran — I thought someone was coming for me and so I ran. I hid up in the woods until I thought it was safe and then I rang you.'

'You didn't see who did it, or who might have chased you?'

Hamlet shook his head.

'And the body's in your cabin?'

'In my study. He's been cable-tied to my chair.'

'And you say his wrists have been slashed?'

'Yes, like with Thomas Midgley and Frank Mooney.'

'Have you touched the body.'

Hamlet shook his head again. 'No.'

'Okay, Dr Mottrell. I want you to remain here with the constable while my colleague and I go and have a look.'

Hamlet nodded and then reached down, picked up Lucky and pulled him close. He began to shake again. This time it wasn't with shock. It was because he had suddenly become aware of how bad this looked for him.

TWENTY-TWO

Two hours later, Hamlet was in custody, stripped down to his underwear, standing on a sheet of paper and having his mouth swabbed and fingernails scraped by a CSI officer. His clothing had already been seized and placed in evidence bags.

As he watched the CSI man place his mouth-swab in a plastic phial, Hamlet started to shake as flashbacks from three years earlier invaded his thoughts. Once again he was the chief suspect in a murder investigation. It didn't help his case that the victim was crime correspondent Kieran Croft, the man who had caused him the utmost mental anguish during these past three years, whom he hated with a vengeance, and who had been found brutally murdered in the study of his cabin.

Before being arrested Hamlet had been subjected to repeated questioning by Detective Constable Nate Fox and his partner, DC Katie Turner, even though he'd carefully explained what he'd seen and heard after finding Kieran Croft dead. He could tell from the tone of their questioning that they didn't believe a word he said and now he was in custody being subjected to an invasive forensic examination.

After signing the labels on the samples they had taken from him, Hamlet was handed a white all-in-one suit by one of the detention officers and he knew what was coming next from his incarceration three years ago.

He wasn't wrong.

Ten minutes later, nursing a paper cup of lukewarm coffee in an interview room, his thoughts were confirmed. He was being interrogated under caution.

Before Detectives Fox and Turner started the recorded interview, Hamlet asked what had happened to Lucky. DC Turner, with a fake, nicey-nicey smile, told him his dog was in police kennels, and that he could take him home once he'd gone through his story again. Her words did nothing to ease the anxiousness Hamlet was feeling, and the look Nate Fox gave him was even less reassuring. *Good cop, bad cop*, was the only thing he could think of as he switched his gaze from one to the other.

DC Turner opened up the questioning, telling Hamlet that the interview was being video-recorded, before cautioning him.

As Hamlet looked across the table at her, he could only think of Alix. They'd had such a good night last night and now this. He wondered if she had told anyone she had been at his place. *Well, I won't be saying anything unless she brings it up.*

The questioning started with Hamlet repeating what he had already told the pair three times already, not deviating once. The two detectives sat poker-faced, locked onto his face as he went back over that morning's events, DC Turner only looking away to write something down in her journal. He tried to see what she was writing but she put an arm around her notes to shield them.

'And you definitely didn't see anyone? Not even the shape of anyone to identify whether they were male or female?' asked Nate.

Hamlet had just finished repeating the part where he'd found Kieran's body and heard the back door bang. He shook his head. 'I didn't see a thing. I thought I heard footsteps, but I didn't have time to look back. All I could think about was what they had done to the reporter, and trying to get away.'

Nate gave Hamlet a disdainful look and said, 'What was Kieran Croft doing in your cabin?'

'You tell me.'

'So, you didn't invite him?'

'Definitely not. I hated that man…' Hamlet pulled himself up, suddenly realising how incriminating that sounded, and quickly added, 'But that doesn't mean I wanted to harm him.'

'Okay, Hamlet. How did Mr Croft gain access to your cabin?'

'I have no idea. The main entrance gate was locked. Padlocked. It was locked when I went down to let you in, after I'd called you.'

'There's no other way to your cabin?'

''Course there is, on foot, but not by vehicle. There's farmland all around my woods, with loads of access. He could have parked up at the entrance to any one of them and walked. Have you checked the lanes for his car? There's a good track just off the main road into Sprotbrough. I'd look there first.'

'That's something we'll be doing as part of our enquiries. Forensics have only just got to work on your place. We haven't started any search yet.' Nate paused, glanced down at some notes in front of him, then lifted his eyes and said, 'Did you tell Kieran Croft where you lived?'

Hamlet let out a bark of laughter. 'You are joking! He's the last person I would want to know where I live.'

'Well he obviously knew somehow.'

'Kieran Croft is fixated on the belief that I killed my family and will do anything to get a story about me. You've seen only recently that he managed to find out about the exhumation. He is a very resourceful man. I can only think that he must have followed me, or followed one of you lot coming to my place.' Hamlet caught his breath as he finished. Alix jumped into his head. *Had Croft followed her last night?* Then he remembered Lucky's reaction when he had been sat on the bench by the stream. *Had the journalist been in the woods, watching him?*

'How do you think he got inside your cabin, Hamlet?'

'Easy. He would have just been able to walk in. The door's never locked. I've never needed to lock it. No one knows where I live. I'm not registered on the electoral register.'

'Are you suggesting that a police officer told Mr Croft where you live?'

Hamlet studied the detective's face. His expression gave nothing away, and in that moment, he strangely reminded Hamlet of one of the many psychopaths he had interviewed over the years, who also lacked empathy. Hamlet quickly shook the thought from his head and answered, 'I'm not suggesting that at all. Like I said, Kieran Croft is a very resourceful man, and I'm guessing his determination to bring me down, even though I'm innocent, has been his goal. He wouldn't have had to work hard at following me. It's not something I've bothered checking, whether I'm being followed or not.'

'You have a real hatred of him, don't you?'

Hamlet couldn't help but smile at the detective's change in tactic. He'd used similar tactics himself during his professional interviews with patients. He responded, 'Of course I hated the man. He carried out a witch hunt against me for three years. But I didn't kill him.'

For the next twenty minutes, Nate covered previous ground, going back over the timeline and sequence of events. Hamlet answered as calmly as possible in order to help with their investigation. Finally the interview ended.

Picking up his notes, Nate said, 'Dr Mottrell, I need to consult with my boss now. You'll be returned to a cell for a short time and then you'll be told what's happening to you. Do you understand?'

'Does that mean I'll be able to go?'

Nate looked at his colleague, DC Turner, and they both shrugged.

That response didn't inspire Hamlet with any confidence and as he was led out of the interview room, back to a cell, all he could think about was what was happening to Lucky.

Hamlet was left languishing in a cell for almost three hours before Detectives Fox and Turner finally came to him.

Nate was carrying a bundle of clothes — jeans, T-shirt and a sweatshirt, with a pair of trainers on top, which he recognised as items from his home.

'We have to keep your clothes from this morning for forensic analysis, so we've got these from the cabin,' Nate said, handing across the bundle. 'Once you're dressed, we'll need a statement from you, and then you'll be released.'

Katie Turner threw him another one of her faux smiles and followed her partner, leaving the cell door open.

Hamlet held back a retort, deciding silence was his best approach. The last thing he wanted was to give them an excuse to lock him up again.

After dressing, Hamlet was taken back to an interview room and for the next hour he again repeated the sequence of events from that morning, whilst Nate wrote it down. The last thing they asked was if anything was missing from his home, and he told them that he hadn't had time to check, and that he would do so when he got home.

'You can't go back home, I'm afraid. Your cabin is now a crime scene. Forensic officers will be there for at least a couple of days,' said Nate, handing him a pen to sign his statement.

Hamlet's jaw dropped, and for a moment he just stared across the table, his mind trying to process what the detective had just said. The cabin was his safe space. His refuge. After a long silence, he said, 'But where am I supposed to go? I don't have any family who can take me in. I've nowhere else to go. That's my home.'

Nate exchanged a bemused look with DC Turner. 'We can suggest a hotel nearby—'

'And are you going to pay for it? The hotel?' he interrupted.

'I know it's not ideal, Dr Mottrell...' said Katie.

'Not ideal,' he snorted. 'Not ideal! Your damn right it's not ideal. This is not my fault. I didn't invite Kieran Croft to my place. He came to my home and unfortunately for him, so did his killer. And yet once again I'm the one who's suffering.' Hamlet could feel his temper rising now. 'Jesus Christ!' he blasted in anger, furiously scribbling his signature at the bottom of each page of the statement before shoving the pages back across the desk.

'I'm sorry about this, Dr Mottrell.'

'Yeah, I bet you are,' Hamlet hissed, pushing himself up from the table. 'Just let me sign for my things and let me get out of here.'

The custody sergeant handed Hamlet his cash, which he carefully checked before putting it in his pocket, much to the sergeant's annoyance. Then slipping on his watch, he signed the necessary paperwork and was shown out of the suite.

Nate followed him out and showed him to the police kennels where Lucky greeted Hamlet like a long-lost friend. He scooped him up, ruffled his head and gave him a hug. At that moment Hamlet felt as though he was going to burst into tears but managed to hold them back, biting his lip as he led Lucky to the exit.

As he was let through the electronic gate by Nate it suddenly dawned on Hamlet that he didn't have his car. The Range

Rover was back at the cabin. He had been brought to the police station in the back of a police car. To compound matters, he hadn't got his coat and it was starting to rain.

Hamlet set off, head down. All he had was £36.40 in cash. His visa and debit cards were back in the cabin. He hadn't even got enough money to rent a room somewhere. At that moment it felt as if the weight of the world was bearing down on his shoulders.

Suddenly, he heard his name being called and immediately recognised the voice. Alix. He looked up and saw a black Audi parked fifty yards ahead. Then a hand appeared through the driver's side window, followed by her head. She waved him towards her. He looked around to see if anyone was watching, but the road was empty. Nate had gone back into the custody suite and so he set off at a jog to the car. The passenger door sprang open as he approached and he bent down to get a glimpse inside the car.

Alix was alone. She said, 'Come on, Hamlet, jump in, you're going to get wet stood there.'

He shot her a puzzled look. 'What are you doing here?'

'Officially, I'm on gardening leave. Unofficially, I'm off the case.'

'What? Why?'

'Jump in and I'll tell you as I drive.'

'Where are we going?'

'My place. I'm guessing you have nowhere else to stay, until forensics have finished with your place? Let's just say I'm returning last night's compliment.'

'But won't you get into trouble?'

'I'm already in enough trouble. They can't do any more to me than they already have.' She revved the engine. 'Now, are you going to get in, or what?'

Hamlet slid in, planting Lucky on his lap and fastening the seat belt. As they set off, he asked, 'Why are you on gardening leave?'

Alix turned at the junction and headed in the direction of Sheffield city centre. 'They found footage on Kieran Croft's mobile of me leaving your home this morning.'

'Shit!'

She nodded, her gaze fixed firmly on the cars in front. 'I can only guess he followed me there last night and waited for me to leave. It's just unfortunate it was this morning. They want to know what I was doing staying overnight with a suspect in a murder investigation. And, of course, it's compounded now by what happened to Croft.'

'But it was all innocent. Didn't you tell them that?'

'Of course I did. Whether they believe me or not is another matter.'

'But I'll confirm it, Alix.'

'I don't think your word will have much sway at this moment in time, Hamlet.' She threw him an apologetic smile.

'But they can't do this. None of this is your fault.'

'The powers that be think otherwise. They say I've compromised the enquiry and so they've sent me home. I've been reported to professional standards and they'll have to conduct an investigation.'

'So what's going to happen to you?'

'I'll keep my job, but it's probable they'll move me from the Major Investigations Team.'

'That is shocking, Alix. I am so sorry.'

'It's not your fault, Hamlet.' She smiled sadly.

TWENTY-THREE

Alix pointed out her house as they drove slowly past a line of Victorian town houses, continuing to the next street junction, which she turned into, driving for a few hundred yards before pulling in between two parked cars.

Hamlet watched her scanning the road up ahead and then checking in her rear-view mirror.

'I'm certain no one's followed us,' she said. 'It's not the kind of thing I'd expect from anyone in my team but professional standards are a sneaky bunch of bastards, and I don't want to make things any worse than they already are.' She glanced in her rear-view mirror again. 'I'm going to let you out here and then drive back to my house. I'll give it a few minutes, check if it's all clear and then give you a ring and you can come over. Okay?'

Hamlet nodded, took a tight hold of Lucky and slowly got out of the car, looking around as he straightened up, even though he didn't know who, or what, he was looking for. Stepping back against a garden wall he let Alix drive away and watched to see if anyone followed her. Then walking back to the junction, he sheltered from the light rain beneath a tree. He was thankful it had eased off because he was there for a good ten minutes before Alix gave him a call telling him the coast was clear. After another quick look around, he made his way along the street to her house, slowing down as he neared her front door where Alix was holding it open, a smirk on her face. She beckoned him with a dip of her head.

'What's the grin for?' he asked, stepping into the hall after another quick look over his shoulder. He saw that the layout, with spindle staircase facing, and doorway beyond leading into the kitchen, was the same as his old house, except on a smaller scale. What he also noticed was how warm the hallway was. Central heating was something he missed in the cabin.

Closing the door, she responded, 'This reminds me of when I used to smuggle in a boyfriend when I was babysitting,' and, letting out a soft laugh, added, 'Take your shoes off and make yourself at home.'

'What about Lucky?' he asked, holding him out.

'Just let him have a sniff around. You're probably going to be here for at least a couple of days whilst forensics are going over your place. He might as well get used to my home as well.'

Hamlet popped him down and Lucky took off towards the kitchen, disappearing through the doorway. Alix followed, leaving him unlacing his trainers.

'I'll stick the kettle on and make us a coffee, and then you can tell me what happened.' Alix stopped at the kitchen door and turned, 'And, before you say anything, Hamlet, this is not a ruse to get a confession. I believe what happened, because I've got something else to tell you about Kieran Croft.'

When Hamlet entered the kitchen, Alix was filling a bowl with water and he watched her set it down on the floor for Lucky who instantly began lapping at it so thirstily that Hamlet guessed it was the first drink he'd had today. Hamlet thanked her.

Alix filled the kettle, switched it on and then turned to face him. 'As well as the video they found of me on Kieran's phone, he had lots more of you.'

'What?'

She nodded. 'It looks as though he's been stalking you. That's how he was at your place. Me turning up must have been the icing on the cake.'

'Christ, Alix. The lengths these journalists will go to get a story. I wouldn't mind but there's not even a story.'

'There is now with him dead and you involved.'

'But I'm not involved.'

'I'm sure his editor won't be viewing it that way, Hamlet. Kieran Croft's name is going to be up there in lights, even in death.' She shook her head. 'And I guess that video of me will be in the digital version of the paper.'

'Are you in a lot of trouble then?'

'Let's just say it's not done my career any good. Lauren was furious when she saw it and she's one of my best supporters.'

'But you told them the truth. It was all totally innocent.'

Alix nodded. 'That's why I'm on gardening leave and not suspended. She has to inform professional standards as a matter of course, and they'll carry out their own enquiry into whether or not I've done anything wrong and if I should be disciplined. The bottom line is, I shouldn't have been at your place on my own, and certainly not drinking wine. Once it gets out that I shared two bottles of wine with a murder suspect, *and then slept over*, what do you think that will look like?'

'But I'm not a suspect.' Hamlet stared at her. 'Am I?'

'Well, it's like I said last night, you are until you're cleared. I don't believe for one minute you killed Kieran Croft, but if you think about it logically, you've had several run-ins with him over the years, especially just recently, and now he's been found murdered at your place and you've no alibi.'

The kettle boiled and Hamlet watched Alix make them both a coffee without saying a word. As she handed him a mug, he said, 'Come on, Alix, would I have rung it in if I'd killed him? No. I'd have dug a big hole somewhere on my land and thrown him in it.'

'Hamlet, it's not me you have to convince, or my boss, or any of my team for that matter. It's what this looks like when it hits the news. And, if it ever gets to court, God knows what a jury will make of it. The instant that video is shown of me leaving your home, just hours before a man is murdered there in similar circumstances to others also being investigated, the prosecution's case is damaged.'

'But why?'

'Because, Hamlet, because,' she answered, her voice raised in frustration. 'You have to understand how this works. The discovery of a body at the home of someone who has been the central suspect in the murders of his family, who has been interviewed and released by the same detective who stayed overnight in the suspect's house just hours before that body was found, is bad. Very bad. Add to that, that the victim is a journalist who has been pursuing the suspect for the past three years and has recently had an altercation with him, and things look bleak, don't you think?'

She stared long and hard at him.

Hamlet responded softly, 'I see what you mean. And you say he's been stalking me? I have to say that doesn't surprise me. I've felt like someone has been watching me on a couple of occasions just recently.'

'I shouldn't really be telling you this, but I'm going to because I believe you're innocent. It looks like he's been doing it for some time. There's footage on his mobile of when you were with me at Thomas Midgley's house, and at Frank Mooney's, and also at the cemetery the other night. I've also been shown a couple of clips of you walking round your woods and sitting by the stream. He obviously had a bee in his bonnet about you.'

'Jesus, Alix,' Hamlet sighed, rubbing his face. 'This is a mess, isn't it?'

'You're telling me.'

After he had drunk his coffee Hamlet asked Alix if he could use her shower. She showed him where the bathroom was and handed him a fresh towel from the landing cupboard. Then, she showed him where he was sleeping. Alix had two spare bedrooms, and after explaining the smallest was used mainly for storage, she directed him to the one at the back, which had a double bed, fitted wardrobes, and was tastefully decorated in lilac and cream, with colour-coordinated bedding.

'You'll have to put up with the colour I'm afraid. Purple's my favourite,' she said, with a wide smile.

'This is lovely, thank you. Purple is good for me. I'm genuinely grateful for this. I know you could get into more trouble if your bosses find out.'

'Right now, I couldn't give a damn. They can shove the job up their arse for all I care.'

'You don't mean that,' he replied, frowning.

'No, you're right, I don't. I'm angry with what they've done to me after all the commitment I've given them. And I'm also angry with Kieran Croft. His actions caused this.'

'And it got him killed.'

Tight-lipped she nodded. 'I'll let you get your shower and I'll rustle us up some food. I bet you're starving.'

'Well, the best on offer in the cells was microwave Spaghetti Bolognaise. The container it came in looked more appetising than the food. Unfortunately, I chose the food.'

Alix let out a brief laugh as she descended the stairs. 'Well, it's chicken salad for tea, and you can like it or lump it,' she called back.

186

The shower felt so good that Hamlet stayed under the warm jets for longer than he normally would before getting out. He changed back into his joggers, T-shirt and sweat top and returned to the kitchen where Alix was cooking chicken fillets in a pan. He thought it smelt wonderful, and could see that Lucky thought the same because he sat as close to her legs as he could get, watching in case something delicious fell out of the pan.

She glanced over her shoulder. 'Five more minutes and this'll be ready. I've done an extra chicken fillet for Lucky.'

'You certainly know the way to a dog's heart. He'll not want to come home, being looked after like this.'

'I've never had a dog before, and never wanted one, but this guy is such a little cutie and I'm getting quite attached to him.'

'He has the same effect on me. Is there anything I can do?'

Alix shook her head, 'The salad is done.' Then, as an afterthought, she said, 'You can pour us a wine if you like. There's a bottle of white in the fridge.'

Alix finished cooking the chicken just as Hamlet began pouring the wine. She chopped one of the fillets into small chunks, made some gravy from granules and presented it to Lucky in a bowl. He set about it as if he had not eaten for days. She placed their fillets among a bed of mixed salad leaves, tomatoes, pineapple chunks, coleslaw and walnuts. It looked mouth-watering. Hamlet handed her a glass of the Chardonnay as he sat at the place Alix had set for him, and, toasting her, took a sip, before setting down his glass and slicing into his chicken. Popping it into his mouth he gave off a long, 'Mmm,' in appreciation.

'Good?' she asked, looking across.

'Beats microwave Spag Bol any day,' he responded, swallowing.

'I'm not sure whether to take that as a compliment or not.'

Hamlet laughed. 'Definitely a compliment,' he answered, cutting another slice.

Alix finished the mouthful she was chewing, took a drink of her wine and said, 'Do you want to talk about what happened this morning?'

Hamlet eyed her for a few seconds and answered, 'Sure, why not.'

For the next ten minutes, he once more recounted everything that had happened, beginning with the walk with Lucky, how he'd returned to find the front door of the cabin open and his furniture disturbed when he'd gone inside. Then, how he'd found his study ransacked, and Kieran's body tied to the chair with his wrists slashed, and finally, how he'd heard the rear door bang, and then ran and hidden before returning back and having a look around before the police came.

'But you didn't see anyone?'

Hamlet shook his head. 'No one. I could hear someone chasing me. Or at least I think they were chasing me. It sounded like it, but I didn't look back. I just kept running.'

Alix nodded. 'And just to take you back, Hamlet; you said the furniture in the lounge was pushed aside. Did it look as if someone had been searching the place?'

Hamlet thought carefully. After a moment, he shook my head. 'No. The first thing that entered my head was that there had been a fight. And thinking about your question, I believe it started in the lounge.'

Alix stroked her chin. 'And you say that the words "You can't hide" had been painted above your fireplace?'

'Yes, and the other piece that's always with it, "Seek, and ye shall find".'

'Do you think it was painted before or after Kieran was killed?'

Hamlet shrugged his shoulders. 'I have no idea. What are you thinking, Alix?'

'I'm just thinking about the scene at Thomas Midgley's and Frank Mooney's. Their bodies were actually in the same room where the slogan was painted. This is different. The killer's signature was in your lounge and Kieran's body was tied up in your study where there was no slogan.'

'Well, I certainly believe I disturbed the killer. What I can't understand, now I've thought about it, is why he gave up chasing me. Once I'd got across the stream, I never heard him. If this is the same person who has already murdered numerous people, and tried to kill me three years ago, then why didn't he stay and try again?'

Alix didn't immediately respond. Her face took on a look of deep concentration. She threw up a hand. 'Two things spring to mind.' She counted them off on her fingers. 'One, he might have thought you weren't alone — that I was still with you. And if that is the case, not only was Kieran Croft spying on you this morning, but so was the killer, and that is very concerning, because it means you are going to have to be especially careful from now on.' She paused and moved to her middle finger. 'And two, the killer, perversely, wanted you to find Kieran's body, and like the other times, he left a clue to further torment you. Did you manage to scan the slogan above the fireplace?'

Hamlet nodded. 'I did, but there was nothing. I checked to see if the app was working and it was.' Pausing, he added, 'Do you think I might have disturbed him before he was able to record it and link it to the website?'

'Did you scan anywhere else?'

'I didn't have time. I had to go down to the gate and let the police in.'

Alix frowned. 'There is a third possibility. Look, we know that Kieran had been following you for some time, not only because he was at the scene of both Thomas Midgley and Frank Mooney's murders, but he also made himself known during the exhumation of Alice Crompton. And now we know, from what I've seen on his mobile, that he also recorded you at least a couple of times at the cabin and he was definitely there this morning because of the recording of me leaving…' Alix broke off and latched on to Hamlet's eyes before continuing, 'Because Frank Mooney was murdered within hours of me visiting him, I've suspected that whoever killed Frank found him through me. It's my belief now that since Thomas Midgley's murder, the killer has been following me. Because of my suspicions I have been keeping a sharp eye out when I've been driving, but it would be fair to say that anyone with a degree of surveillance knowledge could follow me, and, unbeknown to me, I could have led him to your place last night, and just like Kieran, who was staking out your place, the killer was also hiding in the woods watching what was going on. Once I'd left, and you went for your walk, he decided to play a little game with you — leave behind his signature, knowing it would scare the shit out of you that he'd been there without you knowing.'

'And you think Kieran spotted him, and, thinking he had the scoop of the century, followed him to the cabin, disturbed him, and suffered the consequences?'

Mouth set tight, Alix nodded. 'That would certainly explain the signs of a fight.'

Hamlet imagined the scenario. Everything Alix had said fitted into place, and yet something was troubling him. He was thinking that given the amount of blood he'd seen surrounding Kieran's body, that his killer would have had enough time to record his signature hallmark before he'd disturbed him. Leaving the messages seemed to be the whole purpose of the killer's theatres of death. He told Alix his thoughts.

For a few seconds she was silent. 'It's not always been the message he's left that's revealed the clue, Hamlet. At Thomas Midgley's house the clue about Tanya's murder came from a message on a piece of paper on his lap. And before that the clue to his death came from that skull image sent to me in the post. The killer could still send something to me, or you, now he's played his little game.'

Hamlet closed his eyes and replayed the morning's event in his head, slowly going through every movement he took, from the moment he entered the cabin, to stepping from the lounge into the study and finding Croft's body. He ran it through his mind's eye until something rang an alarm. There had been a picture amongst the papers scattered on the floor but he'd been too distracted by the shock of finding Kieran to notice.

His eyes snapped open and locked with Alix's. 'I think there *is* a message for me. And I think Kieran Croft *did* disturb the killer in the middle of leaving it.'

TWENTY-FOUR

'It was one of Helen's drawings,' Hamlet said.

'What?'

'One of Helen's,' he repeated. 'She loved sketching, mainly when we sat out on the veranda during a weekend visit. In fact, one of the last things she sketched was a picture of me at the table outside the cabin. I liked it and framed it.'

'I think I know the one you mean. I remember seeing it on the wall in your lounge,' Alix said.

Hamlet nodded. 'I brought it with me from the house at Arbourthorne when I sold up and moved to the cabin.'

'What about it, Hamlet?'

'It had been taken from the wall. I remember now seeing it on the floor of the study among all the papers. It had been taken out of its frame. He paused for a moment, holding Alix's gaze and then said, 'If your theory is right about the killer leaving a message for us, then I think that's where the message is: I'll find it when I scan Helen's drawing.'

Alix stared at him. 'But you're not able to, Hamlet. Your cabin is a crime scene. It's sealed off until forensics have finished with it.'

'And you can't check either because you're off the case.'

'We have to speak to DI Simmerson and tell her your thoughts.'

Hamlet threw her a look of indignation. 'You are joking. After what they've put me through again, I'll be damned if I help them.'

'But if the killer has left a clue then you have responsibility to share that.'

'Maybe I do. But I'm damned if I'm going to. If anyone's going to find that clue, it's me. And, if there is one, then I'll give it to you. They'll have no choice but to take you back on.'

'It doesn't work like that, Hamlet.'

'In my book it does. I'll go back there later tonight, when it's quiet.'

'But they'll be a guard there. We always leave an officer at the scene to protect it until we finish our work.'

'I'm guessing they won't be actually at the cabin, because it's so isolated and dark. It's my bet they'll be parked up by the gate near to the road. I know lots of other ways to reach the cabin. There are loads of tracks at the top end used by the farmer whose fields surround it. I can park up on one of those and walk through the woods. I know the place like the back of my hand.'

'And how are you going to get there? Your Range Rover is still parked next to your cabin.'

'I can borrow your car,' he replied, offering up a winning smile.

Alix shook her head. 'You are definitely not borrowing my car. I'm in enough trouble as it is. If my car is seen anywhere near your place, I'll not only be out of MIT, I'll be out of a job.'

Hamlet shrugged his shoulders. 'I'll get a taxi then.'

'Hamlet, you are definitely not thinking straight. This could land you in a whole heap of trouble. Tomorrow morning I'll ring up my DI and tell her you've rung me and told me about Helen's drawing. I'll explain your theory and tell her we need your phone to use the app. That will be the best way to handle this.'

Hamlet's face hardened. 'I'm sorry, Alix, but after all that's happened I have a point to prove. I want to clear my name once and for all. And I want to catch the killer. Right now, I really don't care if I get into trouble, I know what I need to do and I'm going to do it.'

Alix let out an exasperated sigh. 'Hamlet, have you listened to yourself, for Christ's sake? A serial killer has found out, one way or another, where you live. He was at your place this morning with plastic ties and a knife. Have you considered the possibility that he could have been there to kill you? Bearing that in mind, it would be advisable not to go anywhere near your place until the killer is caught. I'm not being dramatic when I say you would be putting your life in danger if you go back to your cabin.'

Hamlet mulled over Alix's words. The killer had already tried to murder him three years ago and hadn't succeeded. Perhaps now he was trying again. Yet if he had wanted to kill him, surely he'd had every opportunity when he was out on his walk with Lucky, or he could simply have waited for him to come back to the cabin?

The more Hamlet thought about it, the more convinced he became that the killer hadn't intended to murder anyone that morning. He'd gone to Hamlet's cabin to scare him and leave another message. Why else had he taken the time to remove Helen's sketch from its frame?

Coming out of his spell, he said, 'I've told you what I think, Alix. If I can't plead to your better judgment, let me just ask you this.' He stared deep into her eyes. 'Aren't you just a bit curious to see if he has left a clue or not?'

Hamlet and Alix set off to the cabin just as the sun was setting for the day, taking as many side streets and minor roads as they could to avoid the ANPR cameras. They even disabled their phones to avoid detection. All the diversions resulted in the journey to the woods taking a full hour — twenty minutes longer than normal — though travelling on quieter roads had made it easier for them to ensure that they were not followed.

For the last half mile, Hamlet guided Alix in, pointing out a farm track that led to the outer edge of his land where the ancient burial chamber was. The car bounced up and down uncomfortably on the uneven track, but it was the safest way in to stay undetected, and two minutes after leaving the main road they arrived at a dead-end.

As Alix slowed the car Hamlet pointed out a gap between the hedgerows where he had seen the farmer bring his tractor in to tend to the land. Alix drove through it carefully, reversing back against the hedge, which was tall enough to hide the top of her Audi, and turned off the headlights. For a moment they sat in silence in the gathering dusk, staring out through the windscreen at a copse of trees ahead that was their entranceway to the cabin.

Alix broke the silence. 'Do you still want to go through with this?'

He turned to look at her. 'Do you?'

'We might as well give it a try.'

Hamlet opened the door and immediately the interior light lit up the inside of the car. Alix instantly switched it off, blowing out a loud breath, followed by a short burst of laughter. 'Now I know how villains must feel. My heart is thumping ten-to-the-dozen.'

'Me too,' he replied, stepping out onto the field that was, thankfully, dry, as he only had on his trainers. Alix on the other hand had kitted herself out with walking boots, combat trousers and a dark fleece. Hamlet could already feel the cool night air creeping through the thin fabric of his sweat top.

They closed the car doors as quietly as they could and set off towards the edge of the wood, crouching low as they approached.

As they pushed their way through a narrow gap between some bushes, Alix whispered, 'You lead the way, Hamlet, and once we reach the cabin, if there's no one guarding it, I'll take over.'

Entering his land, Hamlet hadn't anticipated how dark it would be, and as he inched forward, he put down every foot carefully to ensure he didn't trip. It was a good ten minutes longer than he expected it would take before they reached the Neolithic burial chamber. From there they had to negotiate their way across the stream. Thankfully, the water reflected back a little of the light coming through the canopy of leaves, guiding them to where the stream flowed around the rocks. The first rock was about eighteen inches from the bank. Hamlet stretched across a foot and planted it down firmly, testing it was secure before launching across to a second rock. Alix grabbed his sleeve and followed closely. In five strides they were across.

A couple of minutes later they entered the clearing and Hamlet could make out the silhouette of his cabin. It was in darkness and there appeared to be no police guard evident. He stopped and listened, holding his breath. The only sound was a gentle wind in the trees that he associated with the woods at night. Nevertheless, he still waited before making a move, straining his ears. He remained like that until he was perfectly happy there was no one else around. Then, taking hold of Alix's wrist, they stepped forward quickly to where the wood store was, throwing himself against the logs once he got there, listening intently. Thirty seconds later, he whispered, 'It's like I thought, they're guarding down by the main gate.'

Hamlet edged around the side of the cabin, Alix sticking close. At the back door he put an ear to it, and, satisfying himself the cabin was empty, he slowly pushed down the handle and eased the door inwards. 'Do you want to take over?' he said quietly.

Alix tapped him on the shoulder in reply and stepped in front. Plunging a hand into her fleece pocket, she pulled out a small bundle, which she began to separate. 'Put these on before we go in,' she said, handing him a pair of latex gloves and plastic overshoes with elasticated tops to hold them in place.

After kitting themselves out, Alix mounted the steps into the kitchen, where she turned on her torch and cut the beam low across the floor.

Hamlet followed the beam of light, making out a series of forensic metal plates on the floor that led towards the lounge. In between were a series of numbered yellow pyramids. He knew from watching police dramas on television that these were evidence markers.

'Only step on the footplates, Hamlet. That way you won't leave behind any evidence that we've been here.'

Her comment threw him for a second. This was his home. Evidence of him being here was all over the place, and he wondered how forensics would be able to tell whether any trace of him was new or old. And Alix had stayed here only twenty-four hours ago. He was about to say something and then decided against it. Now was not the time. Instead, he watched Alix make her way across the metal plates, and followed, stepping through the kitchen into the lounge. The plates criss-crossed everywhere, and as Alix cast her torch around, Hamlet saw more yellow pyramids dotted around, not just on the floor, but up on the mantel above the fire, and resting on his upturned coffee table and shifted sofa.

'You said you've already scanned this?' Alix asked, setting her beam on the wording daubed across the chimney breast above the fireplace.

In the torchlight the two red sentences looked chilling. Hamlet shivered before gulping out, 'Yes,' the words sticking in his throat.

Alix pulled back the beam, swinging it towards the study, where it rested on the door. Then, stepping across on the metal plates, she slowly pushed open the study door, flashing her torch around as she did so.

Over her shoulder, Hamlet saw the room was in the same state he had last seen it, his desk ransacked, paperwork littering the floor, except now, there was no dead Kieran Croft. The chair Kieran had been tied to was tucked into the corner and the pool of blood had dried, forming a thick dark stain.

Alix danced the torch beam across the scattered papers.

'There!' Hamlet pointed out Helen's sketch, which she spotlighted.

At the sight of his late wife's sketch on the floor, Hamlet felt a tightness in his chest that made him catch his breath.

'You okay, Hamlet?' Alix asked softly.

He nodded, even though he wasn't. All he wanted was to get out of here, but he knew they had to do this.

Alix said, 'You need to reconnect your phone and scan the drawing to see if there's a message from the killer.'

Hamlet took his mobile out of his joggers, clipped the battery back in and fired it up. Selecting the app, he watched it loading and then, crouching down, held the phone over Helen's drawing.

Alix turned off her torch.

Within seconds an image emerged on the screen.

'You were spot-on,' Alix said, placing a hand on his shoulder, excitement in her voice.

The image was of a large, derelict-looking Victorian Gothic house, set over three floors with three attic windows in the roofline. In front was a weed-infested gravel drive.

'Creepy place. Where is it?' said Alix.

As if hearing her words, the picture panned right, back down the gravel drive, where a wooden signboard came into view, the paint upon it grimy and flaking. As the camera focussed in on the name on the board, they both read it aloud at the same time: 'Springfield Children's Home.'

TWENTY-FIVE

Hamlet and Alix quickly made their way back through the woods to Alix's car, all the time looking around, checking they were still alone. The Audi was where Alix had left it, parked beside the hedge. They stopped a moment, probing the dark and listening before climbing in. The only sound was traffic noise in the distance. Hamlet's heart was racing.

Jumping in, they set off back down the bumpy track, driving without headlights for the first few hundred metres until coming to where the track met the road and then Alix turned them on, lighting up the carriageway ahead. She turned left towards the village of Marr to pick up the A1(M) that connected with the M18 into Sheffield. Traffic was light in both directions of the motorway, and they hit Sheffield within half an hour. Here the traffic was heavier and it took them another twenty minutes to drive the three miles across the city towards Totley.

Neither of them had any idea where the former children's home was and they stopped and asked a number of people before a man in his fifties gave them a series of directions through a housing estate half a mile up the road, telling them, 'It's shut down now. No one lives there. It's ready for knocking down.'

Hamlet and Alix answered 'We know' in unison, smiled at each other, thanked the man, and drove away, leaving him with a bemused look on his face. Two minutes later they drove into a 1950's council estate cul-de-sac. At the end they could make out a wide entranceway flanked by two large stone pillars.

Alix slowed to a crawl, powering down her window as she entered the gravel driveway, and Hamlet could see from the way she gripped the steering wheel that she was on high-alert. A few yards in was the sign they had seen in the phone recording, identifying the place as Springfield Children's Home, and seconds later they were pulling up in front of the large house which had double-fronted gable windows and a spectacular mason-carved stone door surround. It had obviously once been a very grand house, probably set in sprawling gardens. Now it was derelict, the windows boarded up and graffiti adorning the walls. Hamlet was surprised it had not been turned into apartments. *Probably too expensive to return it to something decent*, he thought, noticing that most of the guttering had gone, and the walls showed signs of damp, with weeds poking between the stonework. It looked in a sorry state.

Alix turned off the engine and the headlights. For a few seconds they sat in silence in the darkness.

'Well, there's no one here,' Hamlet said in a low voice.

'You mean it *looks* like no one is here,' Alix replied, just as quietly.

Hamlet scanned the front of the building. 'No, I don't think anyone is going to be here. The killer intended for me to see that message this morning and then drive straight over here. That was a good twelve hours ago now. There's no one here, I'm telling you.'

'So what do you intend to do?' Alix asked, her eyes scoping the dark surroundings.

'We should have a quick look around, see if there's anything been left for me to scan. The killer obviously wanted me to come here for a reason.'

'We can wait till tomorrow, when its light.'

Hamlet opened the car door. 'I'm going to take a quick look. You stay here and I'll ring you if I find anything.' He held out his hand. 'Lend me your torch.'

Alix proffered a reluctant look.

'I'm only going to be a few minutes. I'll have a quick scout around and if I find anything, I'll call you. Honest.'

She slapped her torch into Hamlet's hand, keeping a grip on it whilst she locked eyes with him. 'No risks, Hamlet.'

'I'm not brave enough to take risks, Alix. You'll hear me screaming from the rooftops if I'm in trouble.'

Hamlet stepped out of the car. Switching on Alix's torch, he set off towards the house, looking for a way in. At the rear of the building the beam picked out a doorway and he made for it. It had been secured with a metal cover, but part of it had been prised from the frame and he saw that there was a gap just big enough for him to squeeze through. Stopping a moment to listen, he ducked his head, angled his body, and forced himself through the space.

He entered a rubble-strewn corridor with open doors to his immediate left and right and he swung the torch beam into both rooms in quick succession. The room to his left looked like it had once been a dining room. There were a couple of oval tables and at least half a dozen chairs, a couple of them upturned, and a large wall unit covered most of the far wall. The room to his right was the kitchen. Many of the units around the walls had been vandalised, and the floor was spoiled with plasterwork where part of the ceiling had come down.

He moved on and entered a narrow hallway with a staircase. He hesitated, flashing the torch upwards to the first floor. Wallpaper peeled from the walls, some of it hanging over in half-lengths. Keeping the beam fixed on the floor above, he taxed his hearing once more.

Nothing.

Hamlet mounted the first step, his foot crunching over fine debris. More fallen plasterwork. He inched forward, listening intently with every careful step. As he stepped up onto the landing, a scuttling sound ahead brought him to a standstill. He drove the beam in the direction of the sound, where it picked out a rat fleeing into an open doorway.

He let out a soft sigh of relief and set off again. There were five doors along the landing, four of them opening onto bedrooms. Inside each were two metal-framed beds, but no mattresses. The fifth room was a bathroom. He ran the torch beam carefully around each of the rooms to see if the killer had left his signature slogan, but there was nothing.

At the end of the hallway was another staircase. This one was much narrower, and he recalled seeing windows in the roofline in the recording, reminding him that there must be an attic in the house. A sudden feeling of déjà vu visited him, halting his progress. Something about this place was familiar but he couldn't think what it was. Shaking his head, he moved on, carefully climbing the stairs, staying close to the wall — he didn't want to take any chances if the wood was rotten.

Although creaking noisily, the stairs held firm, and Hamlet stepped up onto a narrow landing with a series of doors to his right. To his left were the roof windows he'd seen in the recording, and as he passed the first one, he looked down. Hamlet could see Alix's Audi but he couldn't see if she was in it or not. He quickly flashed his torch through the grimy glass to let her know where he was and then passed on to the first door. It was ajar and he pushed it open slowly.

The first thing he saw was a chair, set at an angle in the far corner of the room. Resting on it was a grey teddy bear. Next to that was a single metal bed. This one had a mattress and a candy-striped pillow. Upon the bed were a couple of dolls, a stuffed panda and a toy giraffe. The bedhead was set against the far wall, where it met the sloping ceiling.

The wall was covered in graffiti. Some of it looked like drawings. Mostly it was scary faces that looked like vampires, and there were a couple of upside-down crosses. What he couldn't miss though was a whole series of the killer's slogans, one above the other. There were at least six of them daubed in bright red paint. Alongside was a group of photographs stuck to the wall. There must have been at least a dozen in total.

Hamlet's stomach started to flutter, but he wanted to see what was in the photographs, and so he inched towards them, the torchlight narrowing and getting more intense as he got closer.

Hamlet stopped. His eyes darted over the images, his brain quickly noting something about each one. They looked to be photos from someone's family album. He could make out a dark-haired woman and a dark-haired man in most of them. In one, the couple were outside a caravan, the woman cuddling a baby. Craning his neck, he saw that it appeared to be the same man and woman in each one.

He could also make out a boy in several of the photographs. In one, there was an infant of about two being cuddled in the woman's arms, the man standing beside her, his hand wrapped around her shoulder. She was smiling but somehow it looked false. The other photos showed the boy in various stages of childhood, up to the age of about ten.

He took a step closer to get a better look. On a second sweep of the photos, he took in not just the people in them, but the backdrop as well. He realised there wasn't just one boy, but two, one a lot older than the other. One of the photographs showed both boys together on a sofa, the older propping up the younger with an entwined arm. The youngest looked to be no more than two and the eldest about ten. The images weren't sharp and had faded with age.

A cold sensation trickled down Hamlet's spine and he could feel the hairs rise on the nape of his neck. Something was gnawing away deep in his mind. Dragging his eyes away he switched his gaze to the toys on the bed and suddenly a flash of recognition burst inside his brain. There was something here that he could identify with but he couldn't put a finger on what it was. Something about his past. He tried hard to grasp what it was, but just as quickly as a memory formed it ghosted away again. *There's one way to find out.*

Hamlet pulled out his phone from his joggers and activated the app. As the screen burst into camera mode, he began to scan the photographs. Nothing. He tried again. Nothing. Then he brought it up to one of the killer's signature slogans. Still nothing. Dumbfounded, he held it over the toys on the bed. Again nothing.

Hamlet was concentrating so hard that he only caught the sound of footsteps behind him at the last moment. He had just started to turn when he felt a painful whack to the back of his head, followed by an explosion of stars, before darkness overcame him.

TWENTY-SIX

As Hamlet opened his eyes a shape emerged in front of him. A fuzzy silhouette at first, and then a face appeared.

James Harry Benson.

Hamlet's heart started to race inside his chest at the same time as the back of his head started throbbing.

'Hamlet! So pleased you could join me. For a moment there I thought I'd killed you.' Benson pushed back the hood of his jacket to reveal dark hair and a bushy beard.

Hamlet tried to search Benson's eyes but they were full of darkness, reminding Hamlet of his sessions with Benson at Moor Lodge.

'Wouldn't be the first time you've tried,' Hamlet replied. His jaw hurt when he talked, and he attempted to reach up to rub it but his arms wouldn't move. He darted his eyes downwards and saw that he had been zip-tied to a chair.

Benson started to laugh.

'You don't have to do this, James,' Hamlet said softly.

'Oh, but I do, Hamlet, I do.'

'Why? What have I done to you?'

Benson sucked in a long breath, swelling out his chest. At six foot three inches — four inches taller than Hamlet — he loomed over him menacingly and Hamlet could feel himself beginning to shake.

'What have you done, Hamlet? What have you done?' Benson repeated, the second time on a higher note. 'Everything! You're as bad as the others.'

Hamlet tried to move his arms, but he was well and truly trussed to the chair. He could see no way out of this. Unless. *Alix*. But then he quickly dismissed that idea. Even if he screamed at the top of his voice, she wouldn't be able to hear him, and anyway, the moment he did that, Benson would kill him. He was in an impossible situation. The only thing he could do was to keep Benson talking and hope that Alix would come looking.

Hamlet said, 'I get it, James. Tanya Johnson and Thomas Midgley lied about what happened at the children's home. Dr Whitton gave medical evidence against you and Detective Frank Mooney was involved in your prosecution. Kieran Croft, well, I guess he was just in the wrong place at the wrong time. But one thing puzzles me — I'm curious to know how you got Dr Whitton to sign your release papers?'

Benson leaned back his head and let out a laugh. 'He never realised it was me at the unit, though I recognised him.'

'I guess that's because you were only fifteen when he gave his evidence. He didn't recognise you.'

'Yes, I realised that,' Benson replied calmly, 'and that's how I managed to play him like I did. He thought I was engaging with him in our sessions. It was good fun to see him lapping up everything I said. And then one day, when he was making us both a drink, I took his phone. By the time he realised it was gone, I was back on the wing and it was hidden. They searched me of course, and my room, several times, but they didn't find it. A few weeks later he quizzed me about its disappearance and I admitted I'd taken it. I told him I'd found child porn on it, which I showed him, and I told him that I'd reveal his dirty little secret to the authorities unless he signed my day-release papers. He didn't believe I'd do it. He tried to call my bluff, so

I sent some of the pictures to his work email. He knew no one would believe him. He was putty in my hands after that.'

Hamlet had wondered how Benson had managed to persuade Ian Whitton to do what he had done, and now he knew. He had never had any doubts that Benson was cunning as well as dangerous and this only confirmed his judgment. He was in no doubt that he was next on Benson's kill list. Unless he could take back control. He had to play along. Massage his ego. Hamlet said, 'But what did Alice Crompton do to you? Everything I've learned about Alice since you gave us that clue would suggest she was fond of you.'

Benson shrugged, and for a second he avoided eye contact with Hamlet. Then he answered, 'She said she was fond of me, but she was just like all the others. She was supposed to be my girlfriend but I found out she was going to some older guy's flat to smoke weed. Midge told me, "Your girlfriend's giving a blow for some blow," and he laughed at me.' Benson paused. 'She betrayed me. And to add insult to injury, she'd said she loved me and wanted to run away with me. When I told her there was no way I would go with her, she said if I didn't do what she wanted she'd tell the detectives that I'd tried to rape her as well.' He shook his head. 'I realised she was no better than the others, and so I strangled her when we were walking through the graveyard, where you found her.'

As he finished talking, Hamlet thought he'd detected a hint of remorse and, latching on, he said, 'But I never betrayed you, James. I was always honest with you. You weren't ready for release. Don't you see that?'

Benson pulled a face. 'This is not just about being released.'

'What is it then?' Hamlet tried to sound calm, though his insides were churning and his head was aching. He tried to think how long he'd been here and if Alix would be wondering what had delayed him. He had lost all track of time. He needed to remain calm. Draw on his training. Keep Benson talking. Pray for time.

Benson flashed a sneer. 'I can see you haven't grasped any of this. Can't you even guess why I brought you here? To show you those photographs over there.' He pointed to the tableau pinned up on the wall. 'And the messages I've been leaving you. "Seek, and ye shall find".'

Hamlet racked his brain but the images still meant nothing to him. He turned to meet Benson's look. His eyes were cold and unfeeling. Hamlet answered, 'They don't mean a thing, James. None of this makes any sense to me…' Suddenly something triggered deep in his subconscience.

Benson clapped his hands together and arrowed a finger straight at Hamlet. 'You do remember something, don't you?'

Hamlet thought for a moment before speaking. 'There's something there now, but I'm not sure what.'

'Don't you recognise the man and woman?'

Hamlet shook his head.

Benson looked disappointed. 'Hamlet, Hamlet,' he said slowly. 'Don't you recognise your own mum and dad?'

The words floored Hamlet. He said, 'My mum and dad?'

Benson nodded, 'Your real parents. Not Robert and Mary Mottrell, Hamlet, but your *real* parents.'

'But…'

'Do you remember what happened to them?'

'I was told they died when I was little,' Hamlet whispered.

'But do you remember how?'

Hamlet was puzzled by this question. He said, 'Sure, I know how they died. I was told by my adoptive parents. They died in an accident.'

James Benson's outburst sounded like, 'Pah!' Then he said, 'Accident! No, Hamlet, they didn't die in an accident. They were killed.'

'Killed?'

'Murdered!'

'Murdered?' Hamlet repeated. 'No … that's not what—'

'Your adoptive parents told you a lie.'

Hamlet shook his head vigorously. 'No. They wouldn't do that.'

Benson nodded. 'They did. They lied to you, Hamlet. And shall I tell you how I know they were murdered?'

'How?'

'Because I killed them.'

Hamlet skin started to goosebump. '*You* killed them?'

'Your dad was a bully. And a child-abuser. And your mum was a worthless piece of shit who did nothing to stop him.'

Hamlet's thoughts were spinning. He wanted to shout and tell Benson to stop. Tell him that he was lying. And yet, somehow, he knew he wasn't. He said, 'You can't have killed them, I was only two and a half when they died. You would only have been…'

'Ten,' Benson interjected.

Hamlet looked at him, dumbfounded.

'Now have you grasped it, Hamlet?'

Hamlet stuttered to get out a response. Finally, he blurted, 'None of this makes sense, James.'

'Do I have to spell it out for you?' Benson said, pointing at the photographs on the wall.

Hamlet started to shake his head, and then stopped and returned a quick nod.

'We're brothers, Hamlet.'

'What!'

'You're my younger brother.'

Hamlet shook his head vigorously. 'No, no! I'm an only child.'

Benson started to chuckle. 'You may think you are, Hamlet, but I can assure you, we are brothers.'

Hamlet sank his head to his chest and groaned. The blood was roaring around his head.

Benson leaned forward and put his fingers under Hamlet's chin, forcing his head up to meet his look. 'You are not an only child. I am your older brother. Our parents were Harry and Dorothy Benson. They were not nice people. Our dad beat me and abused me. Regularly.' He paused, then viciously spat out, 'And Mum let him do it. She would leave the room when he started, and take to her bed, and then return when he had finished to give me a hug and tell me she loved me. Do you know what that felt like, Hamlet?'

'I can't imagine.'

'She might as well have abused me herself. That's what it felt like.'

'But, killing them … how?'

'Easy! Dad was a pisshead. He went to the boozer most afternoons and came home drunk, and mum was doped up most days on antidepressants, or sparked-out on sleeping tablets. I sneaked home from school one day, hid in the pantry and waited for Dad to come home from the pub. He always made himself a cup of tea when he came in, and I watched him from behind the door, waiting for him to go to the toilet. As soon as he'd made his tea, he went for a piss, and while he was in the toilet, I put some of Mum's sleeping pills in his cup. The moment he fell asleep, I got his Stanley knife from the toolbox and cut his wrists, and watched him die.'

'Jesus, James.'

'I got such a wonderful buzz watching him, Hamlet. This man who had abused me most of my childhood didn't have a clue what was happening to him. He never woke up. It was a wonderful feeling watching him bleed like that and seeing him die.'

Hamlet shook his head in disbelief. 'But why your mum?'

'*Our* mum, Hamlet. *Our* mum. I already told you. Because she was such a sad, pathetic creature, that's why. She should have protected me but she didn't. I waited for her to come home and when she found Dad like that, I hit her over the head with a poker. I had to hit her a few times before she died.'

'My God.' Hamlet couldn't believe what he was hearing. 'But what about the police? Surely they came?'

'They did,' Benson answered, nodding. 'I told them I'd seen Dad hitting Mum with the poker, and that I'd run upstairs and stayed in the bedroom with you until the shouting had stopped, and then I came down and found them like that.' He flashed a congratulatory smile. 'The police believed me; after all, I was only ten. Why shouldn't they?'

'Is that how I ended up living with the Mottrells?'

Benson was silent for a moment, studying Hamlet's face. 'That's the one thing I hadn't thought about. What would happen to us. The only thing going through my mind when I killed them was that I was protecting us both. I hadn't thought about what would happen to us afterwards.'

'We were taken into care.'

Benson nodded. 'Foster parents. At first. Then the Mottrells came and took us home. But I wasn't there long. They didn't want me. They said I was a troubled child, and they could only cope with you and so I was sent to the children's home — *this* home!' He swung his arms out violently to indicate their surroundings. Then he said, 'Do you know what it was like?'

'I can't imagine, James.'

'It was fucking awful. I'd cry myself to sleep, and Midge, who I shared a room with, would take the piss out of me. He kept calling me a cry baby.' He paused and said, 'When I did him, it was like killing Dad all over again. He got what he fucking deserved. I got such a high watching him die. Do you know that?'

Hamlet did. It confirmed what he'd known all along. That Benson was a psychopath. Comprehending his need to kill wasn't difficult. What *was* hard to get his head around was that Benson was his brother. Or so he said. He asked, 'But if I'm your brother, James, why did you try and kill me? Why did you kill my wife, Helen? That doesn't make sense.'

'I'll tell you why, shall I, Hamlet? Because I'd protected you, and saved you, and you deserted me. You betrayed me.'

'But that wasn't my fault. I was only two.'

'Yes, but you had your chance to repay me for what I'd done for you. When you took over my assessment in the secure unit, you had the opportunity to save me. All I wanted to do was go out on release. Smell the fresh air again. *Be* someone again. And you refused that request. You betrayed me, after all I'd done for you. I'd given you your freedom but you refused to give me mine!'

'But I didn't know, James. How could I have known you were my brother?'

'Well, you know now, Hamlet, don't you? And this is where we part company once and for all.'

Benson dropped his gaze to his hands, and Hamlet followed them. Something glinted in his grasp, and although he couldn't see what it was, he could guess. He was about to call out, to beg him not to kill him, when a shape appeared in his peripheral vision.

Alix.

She flew at Benson, delivering a solid kick to his chest, sending him flying backwards into the metal bed. Hamlet heard Benson moan as he smacked into it and watched him sink to his knees. Alix landed on her feet and without stopping leapt into the air again, bringing down a fist to the back of his neck. Benson's face hit the wooden floor with a dull thump and he let out a muffled cry. Hamlet watched, fascinated. He had hoped and prayed that Alix would come and rescue him but he hadn't anticipated it happening in this fashion.

Next, he heard a loud hissing sound and caught sight of a steam-like jet shoot from her hand and hit Benson full in the face. A split-second later Benson released a scream and started clawing at his face, rolling into a ball. Hamlet realised Alix had sprayed him with her police-issue PAVA spray, with accurate effect.

Alix delivered a swift kick to Benson's ribs which brought about a moan, and as he rolled away in pain and to protect himself from another, she snatched up the knife and dashed over to Hamlet.

Gripping the chair, he watched her cut the first plastic tie. It fell away, freeing his left arm, and it instantly started to tingle as blood revived the feeling in his hand. She sliced through the second restraint.

'We have to get out of here, Hamlet,' Alix cried, yanking him up.

His legs felt like jelly and he momentarily wobbled.

She caught Hamlet, tightening her grip around his waist. 'Now!' she screamed.

Across the room, Hamlet could see Benson getting to his feet. He didn't need to be told a second time. He clung to Alix, forcing his feet into a run.

They took the stairs two at a time, jumping the last two onto the first-floor landing. Above them they heard bangs that sounded as if the metal bed was being thrown against the wall. Then they heard Benson yell, 'BASTARDS!'

'He's coming!' Alix shouted, between gasps, sprinting to the second staircase.

They both hit those at speed, grabbing the handrail as they flung themselves down.

Hamlet could hear Benson's heavy footfalls behind them. They were crashing down the narrow attic stairway. He'd never been a runner and his chest was starting to burn as he gasped for air. Under any other circumstances he would have pulled up, but fear drove him on. He saw Alix leap the bottom three steps, heading for the rear door.

Alix slipped through the gap easily, but Hamlet hit the metal panel that had secured the back door at a bad angle, jarring his ribs and causing so much pain that all he saw for a second was stars. His legs almost gave way but Alix grabbed his arm, stopping him from falling, and then she hauled him through.

'You okay?' shrieked Alix.

He couldn't reply. He couldn't breathe.

'We have to go,' she roared. 'He'll catch us.'

Hamlet needed no more telling. He clawed in a breath of air, wincing at the pain, and stumbled after her, aiming for the car.

'We haven't got time for the car, Hamlet. Just run!' she bellowed as she fled down the driveway.

Hamlet held his side as he ran, surprising himself that he could keep up with Alix in spite of the shooting pain his ribs. As he reached the entrance, he could hear sirens, and following Alix into the road, her arms flailing in the air to grab their attention, he was relieved to see flashing red, blue and white lights coming towards them.

'I called them right before I came looking for you,' she gasped between breaths, dropping to her knees in the road.

TWENTY-SEVEN

'Here, take this.'

Hamlet looked up from stroking Lucky's head to see Alix holding out two glasses of white wine.

'It won't stop the pain, but it might dull it a little,' she laughed, passing him a glass.

He took it and watched her slump down into the armchair across from him, tucking her feet up beneath her.

'Bottoms up,' she said, raising her glass and taking a long gulp. Then, wiping her lips, she added, 'What a day.'

'You're telling me,' he responded, taking a drink and then flinching. Even swallowing hurt.

Following their rescue, in the form of over a dozen police officers, Hamlet had been rushed to hospital. There, X-rays had revealed that he had two broken ribs. After being given painkillers he had been released.

Alix had been waiting for him, and because he had nowhere to go — his cabin was still a crime scene — she had driven him back to her place. On the way Alix had told him that Benson had been caught and arrested.

The other news she gave him was that he was officially no longer a suspect in his family's murders. He knew he should have felt elated, but he didn't. He was still rocked by Benson's revelation. The man he hated most in the world had told him he was his brother. If that was true, it was going to take some getting used to.

Alix had been studying Hamlet's face. She said now, 'At least you know the truth, Hamlet. Some people don't even get to know that.'

He took another drink, swallowing gingerly, so it didn't hurt as much. He understood where she was coming from. There were people out there who had lost loved ones to crime and never fully knew what had happened to them. He now had the full story, and although he had been given closure of sorts, he also had an overwhelming feeling of guilt. The person who had killed everyone he had ever loved was his own flesh and blood, and, what was more, Benson blamed *him* for their deaths. At least he had the satisfaction of knowing that now they had caught him, he would be going away for a very long time. Probably for the rest of his life.

'At least they have him locked up now, Hamlet.'

He blinked away a tear and looked across at Alix. He suddenly felt light-headed. The wine, together with the two co-codamol he had taken an hour ago, were starting to take effect. His eyes lingered on her face.

She threw him a comforting smile and said, 'Enough of this maudlin behaviour. I don't know about you but I'm famished.'

'Now you mention it, I am a bit peckish.'

'Food it is then.' Alix launched herself up out of the armchair. She downed the last of her wine and set off for the kitchen. 'You can help, if you want. I've got some fish in the freezer and some salad. Not gourmet by any means, but it will keep us going until morning. And I don't know about you, but I could do with another glass of wine.'

Hamlet eased himself out of his chair, 'Thank you for this. I could get used to being looked after.'

Alix threw him a stern look. 'Don't get any ideas, you. Remember, I'm a woman with issues.' Pausing momentarily, she continued, 'Scared of the dark side, we are,' she said in the voice of Yoda from *Star Wars*.

Hamlet burst into laughter, quickly clamping his hands to his sides as a jolt of pain stabbed his ribs. 'Ouch, that hurt. I definitely need another drink to take this away.'

'Well, I'll do the food and you do the wine. What do you say we get wasted and forget our demons for one night?'

Hamlet smiled to himself. It had been a tough journey these last three years but now the healing process could really begin. 'More wine it is then,' he answered and followed Alix into her kitchen, Lucky hot on his heels.

EPILOGUE

Hamlet followed the narrow path in Christ Church Cemetery, glancing at the neat rows of headstones he passed. It didn't take him too long to find the plot, even though his last visit here had been twelve months ago. The grave was tidy, the grass recently trimmed, with fresh flowers in a pot, and he put this down to Helen's parents. Last year, when he came, he had spotted them before they had clocked him, and, so that there was no embarrassment, he had tucked himself behind some trees and watched as they paid their respects and left. Despite being officially cleared of Helen's murder, things were still awkward with her family. And so today, on the anniversary of her murder, he'd waited until early evening before making his visit.

The cemetery was tranquil, the only sound the rustling of leaves in a gentle breeze. It was so peaceful that as he halted before the grey marble headstone, sadness suddenly engulfed him, reducing him to tears. The grief momentarily racked his body, then, wiping away the tears, he read the engraving on the headstone, even though he knew the inscription by heart.

Helen Mottrell
32 years
Beloved Wife and Mother
Also
Much Loved Daughter
Phoebe
Taken by Angels

Their unborn daughter had been laid to rest in his wife's coffin, though he hadn't seen them; he had been on remand in prison when Helen's family had buried them and the police hadn't allowed him to attend their funeral. Even if he had gone, he wouldn't have been made welcome: Helen's family had made that quite clear at the time. *Hopefully, in the near future, I'll be able to heal the bitterness in their hearts.*

Clasping his hands together, he bowed his head reverently and said a brief, silent prayer.

Lifting his head he saw that the sky was starting to turn orange. Day was giving way to evening. It was time to go home. Whispering his goodbyes and blowing a kiss he smoothed a hand across the headstone, caressing the marble and willing for a spiritual connection. There was nothing except sadness, and he pulled back his hand.

Brother or no brother, I'm going to get you for this, James Harry Benson. If it's the last thing I do.

A NOTE TO THE READER

Dear Reader,

I have been toying with the concept of a new series for around two years, working on characters and ideas, and it was a chance encounter at a local charity function meeting Consultant Forensic Psychiatrist, Dr Darran James Bloy, that fired up my imagination and sparked the beginnings of an idea.

Giving me several hours of his time to talk about his role, I got some very interesting material from him and picked up on his laidback quality that I knew readers would embrace. Any liberties taken with facts he told me are mine.

Hamlett Mottrell came courtesy of a Victorian headstone in my local churchyard. What a find.

Placing Hamlet in the right setting was the next thing I focussed on and that came again by good fortune when my good friend Giles Brearley invited me to see some woodland he had bought. Within those woods he showed me a Neolithic burial chamber-cum-shrine that had once contained the skeletons of two of the tribespeople that once lived there, the remnants of a 4000-year-old stone circle, and the foundations of a Roman smallholding. Once I had swapped Giles's wooden shelter for a cabin, I had Hamlet's residence.

Finally, the storyline. I am a detailed plotter when it comes to preparing my books, and I had just made a start on planning the storyline for Hamlet's first adventure, when by chance I got a visit from my journalist friend Graham Walker, digital editor for the *Sheffield Star* newspaper, who wanted to show-off a phone app that had been developed by a friend of his for advertising and promotion. The foundations of it were hinged on using advanced graphics to wow the audience. The demonstration he gave me utilised a glossy brochure produced for a forthcoming ancient Egypt exhibition, the centrepiece being the golden mask of Tutankhamun. He activated the app over an image of Tutankhamun's sarcophagus, and before my eyes the sarcophagus lid floated off revealing the bandaged mummy which unravelled to reveal the face of young King Tut. I was blown away, and just knew I could make use of this, especially putting it in the hands of my psychopathic serial-killer to showboat his killings.

I also would like to thank Alix Rainbow for allowing me to use her name.

Also, a big shout out for the wonderful team at Sapere Books who have given me such expert guidance and support and breathed life into Dr Hamlet Mottrell and Detective Sergeant Alix Rainbow.

Lastly, I thank you the reader, and all the book bloggers and reviewers who have left such kind reviews. Word of mouth is such a powerful thing and without you I would have fewer readers, so, if you have enjoyed this book, would you kindly leave a review on **Amazon** or **Goodreads**. And, if you want to contact me, or want me to appear and give a talk about my writing journey at one of the groups you belong to, then please feel free to do so through **my website**.

Thank you for reading.

Michael Fowler

www.mjfowler.co.uk

Sapere Books is an exciting new publisher of brilliant fiction and popular history.

To find out more about our latest releases and our monthly bargain books visit our website: **saperebooks.com**

Printed in Great Britain
by Amazon

45073338R00126